paper airplanes

a novella

hannah olin

Published by HoppingBird Productions, LLC
ISBN-13: 978-0991261734
ISBN-10: 0991261739

Love me for a lifetime
or do not love me at all.

Victoria Brooks

Dedicated to VRMB.

table of contents

one

An omniscient gloom had settled over the lake, making everything around us grey as we stared out at the gently pulsating water. No one spoke as storm clouds rolled in, threatening to pour rain on our heads. But we didn't care about that; we welcomed the challenge.

We were standing on the pier, wedged between the rear of the aquarium and the waterfront. A thick, twine rope lamely kept us from the shallow harbor below. The pier was empty, devoid of tourists and boaters who all feared the impending storm. It was quiet, save for the wind that blew mist and the smell of fish into our faces.

I looked around me. There were four of us in total, all standing clustered together with our heads bobbing like buoys. Some of us were glancing at our phones, checking the time, answering texts, letting our parents know when we would be home. Others were simply taking in the gloomy beauty of the day, scanning the horizon and breathing deeply, even though our collective sadness weighed our chests down.

There should have been five of us. Wilder should have been with us, breaking the silence with her insensitive jokes or the puns we all hated so much. She should have been rapping a line from a new song she had heard that morning, offering us no context. She should have been illuminating this dreary day with her infectious smile.

We were at the harbor that day because of her. The five of us had spent a lot of our time as friends on this pier. The other places we hung out were the Church Street Marketplace and each other's houses, if our parents were cool with it. We especially hung out at Wilder's house, in her basement bedroom, where we had graffitied the walls we had drunkenly kicked holes in.

But five had turned into four overnight. Wilder was dead. She had been dead for a total of eight hours, and in our unbearable and unfathomable sadness we had somehow decided, via a group chat that still included her number, to meet here, behind the aquarium. It only seemed right. And it only seemed right that today, of all the days in what otherwise was a beautiful, sunny July week in Vermont, it would be storming.

"Does anyone have anything they want to say?" Matt Descoteaux asked sullenly, his eyes locked on the concrete beneath his feet, a finished cigarette dangling between his fingers. Matt was one of Wilder's newest friends, but he was also one of her closest. He was the hopeless romantic of our group, the son of French-Canadian immigrants who found solace in smoking and painting. He had been in denial about Wilder's impending demise for weeks, even after she told him she didn't have very long. And now, in her death, he felt as if she was saying "I told you so" one last time, in true Wilder fashion.

Silence followed Matt's inquiry. Everyone had something to say, a memory to share, anger at how unfair all of this was. But words never quite did Wilder justice. And now, words wouldn't do our grief justice.

"She would be happy we're here," a soft, cracking voice stammered a few moments later. It was Jessa O'Connor, Wilder's neighbor and childhood friend. She had her arms wrapped around herself, the wind blowing long strands of auburn hair so it stuck to her tear-drenched face. Awkwardly, Amari Bender, the tough-as-nails football player in our group, put his hand on her shoulder as her sobs finally became too much. Matt and I looked away, unable to watch her cry like this.

"Fuck," Matt muttered a few minutes later, his tongue pressed firmly into his cheek. I saw him dig his knuckles into his eyes to stop the flood that threatened to make an appearance. Wordlessly, I pulled out another cigarette and a lighter and handed them to him. He nodded graciously.

Off in the distance, somewhere over the lake, the sound of thunder began rolling through the clouds. The first few drops of rain fell on us, and at first, I thought they were just my own tears. But soon, the downpour began, raindrops violently pelting our bodies.

We didn't scamper for cover. We stood and just let the rain drench our heads, cover our faces, soak our pants and shoes and socks. Our jackets kept the rest of our bodies dry, but did little to keep us from feeling the steadily dropping temperature. The lake became choppier, the boats shifting up and down unevenly in the harbor as the waves kicked up.

Another roar of thunder shattered the clouds, this one much, much louder. It sent vibrations through our bodies, the sound waves acting like dull electrical shocks. There was a flash of lightning. And still, we remained.

We must have stood there for half an hour, getting progressively colder and wetter, knowing full well that our parents would disapprove but not caring because right now, nothing mattered. Our senses were becoming numb; we felt nothing other than massive sadness.

"It's almost three," Amari eventually called out over the rain. "KJ and I have to get home." I nodded in agreement. Matt and Jessa looked at us with tears in their eyes, but said nothing. I gritted my teeth and tried not to show how much pain I was in.

Amari and I, neighbors since we were five years old, lived on King Street, which was only a few blocks from the harbor. But we had taken my car anyway, and parked it in the public lot in front of the aquarium. We made our way to the silver Honda that Wilder had named Gordy, trying to outrun the thunder. Amari shot me a glance when I started to open the driver's side door.

"You know," he shouted over the downpour. "Your parents always told you not to drive emotional."

"Fuck off," I muttered. His face softened. I tossed him the keys.

It should have been me. I should be dead right now, not Wilder. I should have died six months ago, but I didn't. Why didn't I? Why did she get sick and not recover but I survived something that should have killed me instantly?

It happened in early January. I had just finished my mid-term exams, and was working late at the Burton store in the Church Street Marketplace. My car was in the shop. Knowing that I wouldn't be done until 10:30 that night, I texted my mom and told her not to worry about picking me up. My co-worker, Travis, could bring me home.

Travis was twenty, a self-proclaimed 'vape connoisseur,' but otherwise a good dude. We had worked together for about three months, and I trusted him enough to drive me the four blocks to my house. We pulled out of the Burton lot and started driving away from Church Street, passing under a green light, when a red pick-up truck with a drunk bastard behind the wheel crashed into my side of the car.

I don't remember seeing the truck approach, or any part of the impact, but I do remember seeing red metal all around me before I blacked out.

When I woke up, I was in the hospital. A doctor was hovering over my bed, telling me I was lucky to be alive. That only one side of my body had been brutally injured, and that the other side—the side with my heart—was perfectly fine. "Not only that," he said. "But despite all the damage to your ribs, your lungs remained unscathed."

I was in the hospital for four weeks. My right leg was in a cast that stretched from my ankle to my thigh, and my right arm was in both a cast and a sling—the bones had been shattered and my elbow was fractured. I underwent two different surgeries to repair my limbs, both of which were successful. And the guy that hit Travis's car was sent to jail.

While I was in the hospital, Wilder came to visit me in my room almost every day. She would sit at the edge of my bed drawing pictures in a notebook she carried with her everywhere, and we would rap along to 2 Chainz until the nurses yelled at us to turn it off. She convinced our other friends to have movie nights in my hospital room, where everybody crowded around my bed with blankets and popcorn and we watched stuff like "The Human Centipede" on Netflix.

When I got out of the hospital, I went straight back to school and work. My parents wanted to talk about the accident, wanted to gauge where I was at mentally, but I told them I was fine and avoided the conversations at all costs. When I wasn't at work, I was at Wilder's house, doing basic chores because she was too sick and her parents were at work so they had a chance at paying her medical bills. On more than one occasion, I helped her siblings with homework. And her mom invited me to stay for family dinners at least three times a week.

I thought about one of the last times I was at Wilder's house for a proper family dinner. It was nearly a month ago, just after they found out there was nothing left for the doctors to do. That every possible treatment had been exhausted. When we found out she was dying. Her mom, Cynthia, asked if I would stay for dinner. Hesitant, I said yes. I sat next to Wilder, across from her mom, and shoveled food into my mouth as her family sat solemnly, picking at their plates. Eventually, Wilder slammed her fist on the table, startling everyone.

"God damn it, people!" she exclaimed, feigning anger that the laughter in her eyes betrayed. "We have a distinguished guest with us, and you are all moping around and pretending like he doesn't exist." Her parents' shoulders sagged. Wilder implored, "Where *is* your hospitality?" Cynthia smiled and shot a look at Wilder's dad, Pete. Pete shook his head, but a small smirk crept onto his face.

Wilder grinned at me before returning to her plate, her head nodding to a beat she was playing in her mind.

Water dripped from my soaked hair onto my lap as I remembered that trademark grin, the one that was so easy to achieve if you made a joke that was just a little bit dirty or morbid. The grin she had on her face when someone told her she was good at rapping. The grin she whipped out when she was trying to make somebody else feel better, even if she felt like absolute shit herself.

I was sitting on the floor in front of my closed bedroom door, staring at the wall across from me. I had changed out of my wet clothes and into a pair of sweatpants and a hoodie, but my hair and cheeks were still drenched. I had no intention of leaving my house again that day.

My mom's worried voice floated upstairs from the kitchen. She was talking to my dad over the phone, who was at work. The words "completely out of it" and "I'm worried, Lou," registered with me, but I didn't contemplate what to do about them. I mean, she was right. I had been out of it when I got home. Not like I was stoned or something, but just dazed. Like Wilder's death hadn't really set in. And maybe it hadn't. Maybe I was just feeling the initial shock of it all, but had yet to really experience the grief that came with losing her.

I'm not sure how long I sat there. But I know my dad got home from work, and my hair finally dried, and I could smell dinner cooking. I climbed to my feet and grabbed a tissue, blowing my nose once to void my emotions. I looked in the mirror, and almost didn't recognize my reflection. There were dark circles under my eyes, and my hair was splayed in all different directions. There were red splotches on my cheeks from where tears had made their mark. I quickly went to the bathroom and splashed cold water on my face, trying to get rid of the evidence.

I walked downstairs and into the kitchen, where my parents were anxiously waiting for me. My mom's face was contorted with what I could only assume was concern and my dad was looking at me like he expected me to burst into tears at any time. I nodded at them and forced a half-smile.

"What's up?" I asked, cringing at my own voice crack.

"Oh, honey," my mom said, rushing to give me a hug. I hugged her back and blinked to keep the tears at bay.

"Mom, I'm fine," I lied quietly as she pulled away, scrutinizing me.

"Are you really?" she asked. I shrugged.

"Well, no," I explained slowly. "I mean, I am really sad she's gone. She was my best friend. But I'm handling it."

My answer seemed to just barely satisfy both of my parents. They each told me that they were there for me, and that they loved me, and how sorry they were that I had to go through this. I nodded and smiled and escaped to the living room, where my little sister was watching TV.

Meadow was thirteen and nosy as hell. She knew everything there was to know about me, whether I had told her or not. I found it was easier to tell her stuff because that way she couldn't get it twisted, because I knew she would figure it all out on her own anyway. But Wilder was the one enigma Meadow had never been able to solve.

Within two minutes of me sitting down in an armchair across from the couch, Meadow had started her inquiry. Her voice was soft, her words carefully chosen. She had been thinking about this for a while now.

"You were pretty close with Wilder, huh?" she said. I nodded and locked my eyes on the television. Meadow continued. "Did you, ya know, have a crush on her?" I smirked and shook my head.

"We were just friends," I explained. "I was like a brother to her. She had a lot of crushes, but I was never one of them."

"Yeah, but did *you* have a crush on *her*?" Meadow demanded, nitpicking my use of syntax. I glanced at her.

"No," I told her. "I loved Wilder, but not in a romantic sense. Why does it matter, anyway?" Meadow shrugged.

"Just wondering." I shook my head.

"You're too nosy,"

"I just like to be informed."

I didn't check my phone until after dinner that night. I had dozens of messages waiting for me, half of which I didn't even read. I checked to see who they were from, but I didn't read the actual messages. I was exhausted, and I just didn't want to talk to anyone, really.

But I had one message from Wilder's mom. Cynthia had written, "Hey Knox. I was wondering if you would want to have a part in Wilder's memorial. I know how close you two were and was just checking to see if you would be up for it."

My initial reaction was *fuck no*. I wanted nothing to do with Wilder's memorial. Hell, I didn't even want to *go*. I didn't want to bury her. I didn't want to say goodbye. What I really wanted to do was run as far as I could for as long as I could, and then when I couldn't run anymore, just curl up and disappear forever. That's what I wanted to do. I didn't want to give a eulogy. I didn't want to be a pall bearer. I didn't want to hand out the little brochures that told people the order of events.

But then I thought, *how fucked up is it that you don't want to go to your best friend's funeral?* If I had died in that car accident back in January, Wilder would have been at my funeral. Wouldn't she? Or would she have been too sad? *Get over yourself*, the voice in my head shouted. *She would have been there to say goodbye, to support your mom and dad and Meadow. She loved you just as much as you love her. So suck it up, you punk ass little bitch, and help her parents out with her memorial.*

I texted Cynthia back. "I'll do whatever you guys would like me to do." I knew that was a dangerous response, because chances were I would be too sad and emotional to do anything of use. After a few minutes, Cynthia replied. "Would you be interested in saying a few words? Nothing major, just something on behalf of your friends?"

Fuck.

two

The purpose of telling someone that they're dying is, in part, so they can plan for their death. They can cross things off their bucket list, give heartfelt goodbyes to their loved ones, settle their debts, get right with the Lord or whatever, and help organize their own funerals.

Wilder was probably the least helpful dying person there was. She didn't make a bucket list because it was too morbid, even for her taste. She didn't really say goodbye to anybody, at least not that I know of. She made plans to see people that she didn't see on a regular basis, but no goodbyes were muttered. Just gleeful 'see you laters,' as if she wasn't rapidly declining. And she didn't comment once about her funeral. Anytime her parents tried to initiate a gentle conversation about it, she would make some snarky comment and effectively avoid it. A social worker described it as "deflecting," a coping mechanism of some sort. She also said that Wilder was in denial about her impending demise, which I told her was bullshit. Wilder wasn't in denial. She had accepted it more than any of her friends had. She just felt differently about it.

So when Wilder died, nobody really knew what she wanted out of a funeral. Her parents wanted it to be less of a funeral and more of a 'celebration of life.' They wanted to remember Wilder and her crazy personality, not her illness. Most of all, they wanted us, her friends, to be at least somewhat happy while remembering her.

The next day, after I got Cynthia's text, I found myself with my friends in Wilder's room. Amari and Matt were sitting on her unmade bed, while Jessa sat at her never-used-for-homework desk and I remained on the floor, which I guess is probably a metaphor for my existence or something.

We were supposed to be writing a quick eulogy for me to read out loud in front of Wilder's extended family and friends. I say we were "supposed" to be writing the eulogy because we hadn't actually written anything. We were just sitting there with only one light on, barely illuminating her graffitied walls, not really talking to each other. But we weren't ignoring one another, or scrolling social media on our phones. We were just sitting, taking in her room.

Wilder's parents were unconventional in the way that they raised her. They were really lenient, never the type to yell when they got mad, and they wanted her to be as creative as possible. So when she was about six years old and told them she wanted to be an artist, they bought her paint and let her splatter it however she wanted on the walls of her bedroom. As a little kid, the paintings were cute and fit society's norms. Flowers with smiley faces on them, rainbows, poor attempts at unicorns, the usual little kid stuff. But as she got older, started smoking weed and began to rail against society, she painted over the conventional shit. You couldn't see the flowers any more under the spray painted "COURTNEY KILLED KURT" conspiracy anthem, and the unicorns had been turned obscene with middle school-style dicks and a competition to see who could come up with the most nicknames for marijuana.

You're probably thinking that Wilder was some kind of stoner degenerate, and maybe you're right. She smoked weed, she got drunk most weekends, and she was only seventeen. But she was also fighting cancer. She had been diagnosed with stage IV neuroblastoma on April 10, 2012, when she was fourteen: before the weed, back when she was still drawing daisies and rainbows. And immediately, she was told she was going to die.

Neuroblastoma is a form of childhood cancer that develops in nerve tissue, typically in the adrenal glands or abdomen. Patients are usually diagnosed between the ages of birth and ten years old, but most diagnoses happen by age five. It's very rare for a child older than ten to be diagnosed with neuroblastoma. Yet that's the kind of cancer Wilder had.

The doctors at the University of Vermont didn't have very high hopes for Wilder. She was too old for any trials because no researcher wanted to use her as a patient. Her age made her an outlier, and any results they got from her would alter their overall findings. So her team at UVM sent her to Sloan Kettering, a hospital down in New York City that was famous for treating neuroblastoma. She took a cocktail of drugs that should have put her in remission, but they didn't work. So she went back to UVM and was pumped full of more chemicals, and she took a bunch of alternative medicines like herbs and juices, and started smoking weed to help with the pain and to get her appetite up. After fourteen months, on June

27, 2013, she was declared NED—No Evidence of Disease.

And because she had been on so much stuff all at once, nobody knew for sure what had done it. So they kept Wilder on a low-dose of chemo for "maintenance," which she joked about on a near-daily basis, and she kept smoking weed. And we all got drunk a few nights after she was declared NED to celebrate. We were fifteen at the time.

The maintenance chemo Wilder was on wasn't nearly as harsh as the stuff they had used to eradicate the tumors, so her hair started growing back. She had her port removed. She started planning for the future.

And then, after nearly two years cancer free, Wilder relapsed. It was April 28, 2015. Eighteen days after the three year anniversary of her diagnosis. She went back to New York City, underwent a six hour surgery to remove the tumors, and when she returned, was ready to fight the disease with everything she had. And she did.

They had to act fast and brutal. The doctors gave her chemotherapies so toxic Wilder spent more time lying on the floor by the toilet than in her hospital bed. They blasted her body with radiation so often that she didn't bother washing off the permanent marker indicating where the technician should aim the laser. Her immune system was shot to hell, meaning we couldn't visit her when she needed us the most. We could only stand outside a glass window that looked into her room, our noses pressed to the glass as we told her about what was going on at school.

And after all of that, after everything she had been through—all the drugs and lasers and needles—she went in for an MIBG scan that everyone hoped would remain dark. If it was clear, she was eligible for a stem cell transplant that would effectively restart her body so, in theory, the cancer wouldn't come back again. The day she was to get the results, June 15, we all sat in her bedroom, kind of like we were now, laughing about how if cancer was a person, they would be all busted up and bruised and pathetic looking, because Wilder kicked its ass so hard.

And then Cynthia walked in. And we all looked up at her with hope in our eyes, and she smiled a tight-lipped smile and told Wilder that she needed her help upstairs. And Wilder stopped grinning and said, "Okay, I'll be there in a second," and Cynthia left. And Wilder looked over at all of us, and we knew.

"I'll be right back," she said, her voice soft as she climbed to her feet, which were bare because she wasn't really a sock person. And she left us in her room, and we all sat there, stunned. And then one by one, we each started to cry. Small tears, because we didn't want it to be true. But we all knew what it meant.

Wilder had told me, right before her scans, that if the cancer hadn't cleared, if she was just as sick or sicker than she was when she relapsed, that there would be nothing left. She wouldn't get the stem cell transplant, and every other option had been tried and used so many times that the treatment would end up killing her before the actual cancer. And of course, I told the others that. Because even though none of us were really all that religious, I figured if we were going to pray, we should pray then. Pray that her scans would be clear. Pray that there would be something left.

But when she left us in her room that day, our doubts that some ever-loving God existed were reinforced.

We got ourselves together, told each other to stop crying because we couldn't let Wilder know we were upset. And a few minutes later, she came back, sat down in front of us with her legs criss-crossed, and grinned. She grinned at us like she had just won the lottery. But we weren't fooled. She looked at each of us in turn, grinning the most pure smile you could ever imagine.

"You guys are such dorks," she finally said, giggling. We didn't react.

"Well?" Amari, who has never been good at handling his emotions, said impatiently. Wilder's grin froze, and she glanced at the carpet beneath us.

"Yeah, nothing worked," she admitted almost casually, her voice steady and calm, as if she was just telling us she failed a math test. "I've got an appointment tomorrow with the oncologist and hospice."

We all started talking at once, demanding to know if there really was no trial in the world for her to take part in, wanting to know how much time she had, and how was she handling the news? Wilder put her hands up, and the grin returned, softer this time, less sure of itself. She contemplated what to say. Eventually, she just said:

"I love you guys."

That was a little over one month ago. Now, I glanced up from my spot on the floor, across the room from Wilder's bed. On the wall above Matt's head, sprayed in forest green, was the phrase "I love you." Wilder's ex-boyfriend had done it several months before, and she had never painted over it. Not because she still had feelings for him, but because it was a good enough sentiment. In a room that was otherwise covered in obscenities, Wilder liked having the contrast.

"We've gotta get started on this eulogy," I said, breaking the silence of the room. Matt and Jessa nodded in agreement. Amari sighed.

"The problem is that Wilder can't be summed up in a couple of paragraphs," he argued.

We lapsed into silence again. He was right. There was no string of words powerful enough to encompass Wilder's entire being. And to only highlight parts of her would be doing her a disservice. She was a walking contradiction, with a personality that had been haphazardly thrown together to create a wild and unapologetic individual. She was an enigma and an open book. She was kind and she was defensive. She was bold and daring, but she was also sensitive and empathetic. She did not give one shit about society and its expectations, or what anyone else thought of her. But every day, she told the people she cared about how much she loved them.

Maybe that's why she didn't say goodbye to anybody. Not because she was too sad or too scared of dying, but because she didn't feel the need. If you knew Wilder, you knew how she felt about you because she told you. She told you if she liked you, and she told you if she hated you. You knew if she wanted to be around you, or if she only wanted to see you again in hell. Wilder left no doubts in anyone's mind. Life is too short to put up false hopes.

Today was only Tuesday, and her memorial wasn't until Sunday. Her parents had decided to delay the memorial to accommodate their extended family's schedules, so we had plenty of time to put the eulogy together. We spent another hour or so in Wilder's room before I left to go to work, and the other three went to get something to eat.

*　　　*　　　*　　　*　　　*

The Burton Company started out as a snowboard manufacturer, but as its brand grew, it expanded to include shoes and other apparel. The location here in Burlington was on the outskirts of the Church Street Marketplace, just a block from the "In-Line Scoop Shop" Ben &

Jerry's where I would have been guaranteed a job.

My parents own the Church Street Ben & Jerry's, having purchased it back when I was nine years old. I essentially grew up in that store, which led to me having an aversion to ice cream. It's not that I don't like eating ice cream, it's just that I've seen too much of it and have nightmares of getting trapped in tubs of the product.

It also led to me having an aversion to my parents. And again, it's not that I don't love my parents, but I'm a rebellious teenager and I don't want my parents to be supervising my every move. When I got to be fifteen and started looking for a job, they of course wanted me to join their team. I politely refused, cleverly using the excuse that I didn't want to be handed my first job. So I worked at a restaurant on Church Street washing dishes, but then someone told me Burton was hiring and offered a discount to its employees. I had been working there for almost a year when Wilder died.

I took a few weeks off when Wilder went into hospice care. My manager was very understanding—it helped that Wilder had been a regular at the store—and found people to cover my shifts. I started going back to work the week before she died. Wilder had asked me to, knowing that I was missing multiple paychecks to spend time with her. But I spent most of my time in between shifts at her house, especially when she was confined to the couch or her bed.

I felt pretty okay going to work that day, thirty-six hours after her death. I parked Gordy in the back of the parking lot behind the shop and took my time walking across the pavement to the loading door. It was a beautiful day, with no evidence of yesterday's storm in the clear blue sky and brutal heat.

Once I was in the store room, where we kept all of our inventory and recycling, I slipped my lanyard over my neck. It had my name tag pinned to it, along with my car and house keys and a couple of keychains that I had gotten over the past two years. I ducked through the doorway and onto the floor, which was considerably busy for a Tuesday. A family of tourists—a mom, dad, and two boys—and a college-aged girl were browsing the racks.

"What's up, KJ," Nate Lowry, one of my favorite co-workers, called from the register. I picked up a T-shirt that had been lying on the ground and folded it up before putting it back on the shelf. I nodded to Nate as our manager walked in from the street.

"KJ," Andrea said as soon as she saw me, rushing past the customers to give me a hug. "I am so sorry."

"Thank you," I said earnestly, returning the hug.

"Is there anything I can do?" she asked, holding me by the shoulders to look at me in the eyes. I tried to smile.

"Just give me a paycheck at the end of the week." It was a weak attempt at humor. Andrea looked at me sadly and nodded, and I started to work. I took inventory. I folded clothes. I reorganized the shoe display. I helped a skier heading to Switzerland pick out new boots.

On my break, I went out to the parking lot and stood under the shade of a willow tree as I smoked a cigarette from my pack of Marlboros. I wasn't a big tobacco smoker—this was only the second pack I had ever bought in my life, and I hadn't ever finished an entire pack by myself. I handed out cigarettes to whoever wanted or needed one. You would think having a friend with cancer would turn me off from smoking, but there was something comforting in holding a lit cigarette in your hand. It was the same thing with a bottle of beer. It just made you feel better holding onto it.

The loading door opened and I glanced over my shoulder to see who it was. Nate's shift had ended, and he was heading out for the day. He strolled over to me, his hands shoved in the pockets of his chinos as he admired the mural on the brick building across the street.

"How you holding up?" he asked me, squinting in the sunlight. I shrugged and took a drag from my cigarette.

"Been a whole lot better," I replied. He nodded understandingly.

"I just wanted to say," he began, but quickly paused. He glanced at the ground, unsure of himself. Finally, he continued, "If you ever need anybody to talk to, I'm here. I lost my aunt to cancer a few years back, so I know what it's like."

"Thanks, man, I appreciate it," I said. And I meant it. Nate nodded again.

"Keep your head up, kid." He patted me on the shoulder and started to walk away.

"Kid?" I called after him as I stomped out the cigarette. He grinned at me over his shoulder. He had just turned twenty-two and liked to think of himself as a fully grown adult, which was total bullshit given he had a baby face and still acted like he was in high school.

The rest of my shift went by quickly. We closed up the store and reset the floor for the morning crew. I got into my car around 10:30, and sat for a few minutes behind the wheel with the engine still off and my mind spinning. I felt something grip my heart, seizing it and sending a knot like the tumors that filled Wilder's body into my throat. I turned the car on and somehow drove it home. But after I parked on the street, I didn't go into my house.

I went next door to Amari's and slipped in through the back door. Neither of us spoke as he grabbed a hoodie and we ducked outside. Weaving through backyards and in between darkened businesses, we eventually arrived at the vacant University of Vermont campus. In the summertime, it was the perfect place to kick it and chill because there usually wasn't anyone around except busy summer students. We definitely abused the emptiness of the campus, using it as a place to crack open beers or light up.

Amari produced a small baggie from the pocket of his hoodie and started rolling a blunt. We were standing in the shadows of the student center, which was illuminated by a couple dim lights that were left on year-round in the hallways.

"Light," Amari demanded. I pulled out my lighter and flicked the trigger so the flame touched the end of the blunt. Generously, Amari handed it to me so I could take the first hit.

Our highs started to peak around midnight, and that's when we began walking home. We hadn't spoken really. We had just sat on the concrete sidewalk, passing the joint back and forth, taking in the clear night and letting our minds wander away from reality. The knot in my throat had left for the time being, but something in me indicated that it would be back eventually. Amari and I muttered goodnight to each other, and I quietly crept into my house, careful not to wake up my parents or Meadow. I made myself a ham sandwich and took it up to my room with a bottle of iced tea, and I quickly downed both before passing out on top of my bed, still in my work clothes.

three

"Knox Fisher,"

Mrs. Holloway glanced up from the roster and scanned the crowd of twenty students before her for a raised hand. But I kept my arm on my desk. Instead, next to me, Wilder raised hers. I tried to hide my smirk as the kids around us glared in confusion.

"Here," Wilder announced, stifled laughter shaking her voice. "I go by KJ." Mrs. Holloway looked at her incredulously from over the top of her reading glasses.

"Rachel Gallon?"

Under our desks, Wilder and I fist bumped.

For as shitty as having cancer was, Wilder knew how to have fun with it. She had peach fuzz for hair and didn't give a flying fuck about gender norms, so she could easily pass for a guy on the days when she dressed in her brother's old t-shirts and went without make up. And on the first day of junior year, that's what she did.

Wilder and I, if you haven't figured it out by now, were extremely close. I'm talking like I was essentially her parents' fourth child. I'm not exaggerating, either—sometimes they'd go out to dinner and make reservations for six, knowing that I'd probably be joining them.

So when Wilder came up with the idea of swapping identities for our second period health class, I didn't think twice about it.

And when Mrs. Holloway called out, "Wilder Murray," I raised my hand and innocently replied, "Here." She didn't bat an eyelash, given Wilder's arguably unisex name.

For an entire semester, no one told Mrs. Holloway who we really were, since by junior year pretty much everyone in our grade knew Wilder was always up to something. Even when Wilder stopped going to school because she was too sick, I kept up the facade for her. It wasn't until the end of the school year, when Amari, Jessa and I put together a fundraiser for her family, that Mrs. Holloway realized our true identities. She wasn't really angry about it, just confused.

No one at Burlington High School knew Wilder was dying. We got the news during finals week, which she was exempt from since she hadn't been to school in months. The classmates Wilder knew would be hurt by her death were informed during her last week. That was her choosing; she wanted to spend the rest of her time with her closest friends and family, rather than fielding text messages and poorly worded well-wishes.

But the news spread pretty soon after her death, and we started noticing an odd phenomenon. Our peers flooded her Instagram and Facebook page, leaving comments like, "Fly high, you will be missed," or "Omg I miss you so much," or "Rest in peace." And while I'm sure these people meant well, Matt, Jessa, Amari and I couldn't figure out why they were commenting on this dead girl's page. It's not like Wilder would ever see them.

"Maybe it's to show support for Wilder's family," my mom reasoned when I brought it up at dinner. I shrugged. It just didn't make any sense to me.

*   *   *   *   *

As a kid, I was ridiculously shy and didn't make friends very easily—Amari was really my only friend in elementary school—so while other kids were out playing flag football or having sleepovers, I was up in my room learning how to play different instruments and reading comic books.

By the time I entered sixth grade, I had taught myself how to play the guitar and knew a few songs on the piano. In third grade, I had picked up the clarinet in the school band for whatever odd fuck reason, and had mastered it pretty well.

I met Wilder on the first day of sixth grade, when I reported to the Edmunds Middle School band room after the dismissal bell rang. I was storing my clarinet in there, since I had no intention of practicing at home. Most of what the teacher was having us do I had already learned and gotten good at, so I wasn't worried about rehearsing outside of school.

Wilder was in the band room that afternoon, talking to a music teacher about joining the choir. When I walked in with my clarinet case, she looked me up and down, and I immediately stopped making eye contact. Like I said, I was painfully shy.

"What instrument do you play?" Wilder asked, cocking her head to one side. I started to scream internally, hoping that I wouldn't have to participate in a real conversation that day.

"Clarinet," I mumbled, shoving the box into a cubby that the band instructor had marked with my name. Wilder squinted at the permanent marker staining the swatch of masking tape.

"KJ," she read. "What's it stand for?"

"My name," I said, wanting to die. She smirked. My anxiety was evident.

"And your name is?" I looked at her, and for the first time since like, I was born, I didn't feel as though this other person was a judge looming over me, about to destroy my entire existence with a snap of their fingers.

I looked at Wilder and saw a fellow human being. And suddenly, I wasn't scared anymore.

"Knox Jameson," I answered, wanting to die a lot less.

"That's a really stuck-up name," Wilder said, a big, mischievous grin spreading across her face. "No wonder you go by KJ." I nodded in agreement, a small smirk tugging at the corners of my mouth.

"My name's Wilder Sage," she told me, balancing the scales. "Weird, I know."

"It's not weird," I said, a little too hastily. "It's cool. I've never met anyone named Wilder." She rolled her eyes.

"No one has. It isn't really a name. It's a comparative adjective." I didn't know what a comparative adjective was at the time—we hadn't learned about those in grammar yet—

but I didn't let Wilder know that. She was more confident than me, and obviously smarter, too. I wanted her to think I was closer to her level, so I tried to play it cool.

We became fast friends from that point forward. Teachers often commented on how strange our friendship was, given we were complete opposites at first. But as time went on, I started to adopt some of Wilder's traits, like her boundless sarcasm and dislike for authority. And then teachers started commenting on how disruptive we were, and how we would be disappointments in high school.

But we didn't care. We were partners in crime. The comparative adjective and the grandiosity-hiding nickname: an unlikely but unstoppable duo.

four

Sunday morning, I woke up early. I took a shower and ate my cereal slowly, dressed in a pair of gym shorts and an old summer camp T-shirt. My mom made coffee while my dad read the newspaper. Meadow sat across from me with the comics section while heaping cereal onto her spoon.

After breakfast, I went back upstairs, my feet feeling like lead. I took my time putting on the suit my mom had ironed for me, gazing at my reflection in the mirror as I tied my tie. White shirt, red tie, black jacket, black trousers. Hair slicked back. I looked sharp, like I was ready to meet the Queen of England or something. But instead I was going to my friend's memorial.

"You look marvelous," my mom said when I walked into the kitchen.

"Thanks," I replied, but the word tasted sour in my mouth. "I'm going over to Amari's for a minute." I didn't wait for a response, I just ducked out the door.

Amari was already dressed when I walked into his house. I said hello to his parents and we went up to his room for some last minute preparations for the eulogy I was giving.

And by preparations, I mean we slid his window open, removed the screen, and lit up.

"To Wilder," Amari said, holding the joint between his index and middle fingers, putting it up in front of the window.

"To Wilder," I responded, my voice cracking from an apparent lack of puberty, not emotion. I touched the flame to the end of the blunt. Amari took one hit and handed it over to me.

"You need this more than I do," he explained. I nodded in agreement.

Even after I finished smoking, my hands still felt clammy and the knot in my throat remained in place. I used some of Amari's cologne to make sure any traces of marijuana were masked, and then went to get in my parents' car.

Wilder's memorial was being held at St. Mark's, a church up the street from our high school. When we arrived at the church, the parking lot was packed with family and friends of the Murray family. For as close as I was with Wilder, her parents and her siblings, I still felt out of place, as if I didn't deserve to be there.

I climbed out of the car, the smell of freshly cut grass smacking me in the face. I glanced over my shoulder and saw Amari and his parents pulling into the lot. Looking towards the church, I could see Matt and Jessa waiting for us on the sidewalk.

"You guys go on ahead," I told my parents. "I'll be there in a second."

Amari and I walked to the sidewalk to join Matt and Jessa. At first, none of us spoke. Amari gazed at some obscure point at the edge of the parking lot, while I shoved my hands in my pockets and watched an ant crawling on the concrete. Jessa absentmindedly braided her hair, sniffling occasionally. Matt searched his pockets for his pack, and I noticed when he went to light the cigarette, his hands were shaking.

"Is Emily coming?" I asked him. He shook his head.

"We're on a break," he muttered distractedly as he blew smoke out of his nose. Emily was his girlfriend, a third-year UVM student that lived in Massachusetts. They had been on-again off-again for most of their eight-month relationship. But even when they weren't technically together, Emily still hung out with us, and she had gotten to know Wilder pretty well. Amari and I exchanged uncomfortable looks—we had both assumed she'd make it to the memorial.

"Should we go in?" Jessa asked, shifting her weight nervously. I took a breath and nodded. None of us were ready for this.

*　　*　　*　　*　　*

The summer before eighth grade, my and Amari's parents hosted a backyard barbecue and invited most of the residents surrounding the Church Street Marketplace. We opened the fence that separated our yards and people filled up the space, filtering in between the houses. The adults were all laughing and drinking beer while the kids chased each other with water guns and shrieked with amusement. Of course, as thirteen-year-olds, we were too cool for that.

Wilder, Amari, Jessa and I stood in the back of my yard, leaning against the fence, hating on the party. Wilder had swiped her dad's beer, and we had split it between the four of us by pouring it into red Solo cups. We felt rebellious and carefree, completely unaware that eight months later, Wilder would be diagnosed with cancer.

As scrawny, freshly minted teenagers, our tolerance for alcohol was a mystery. It was my first time drinking beer, so I thought I felt tipsy off my quarter cup. But in reality, it was probably a placebo effect, because I don't think anyone has ever gotten a buzz from a quarter cup of beer.

That said, we thought we were hot shit for getting mildly intoxicated in front of all these adults. Wilder's mom saw us laughing uninhibited by the fence and came up to us, enthralled by our visible display of friendship. Like all parents, she got a high from seeing her kid forming bonds with her friends.

"I just need to take a quick picture," Cynthia crooned, and immediately, we all groaned.

"Mo-om," Wilder rolled her eyes. Cynthia ignored her and pulled out her phone, directing us to get in close. Wilder's eyes were still in the back of her head, so I made some dumbass joke that, if Cynthia had really paid attention to, would have completely given away the fact we were drinking beer.

The joke would have been high risk if Cynthia wasn't so unsuspecting, which made Wilder's jaw drop and break into a huge smile.

"You're an ass," she laughed. Proud of myself, I swung my arm over her shoulder and stuck my tongue out. Amari had his hand behind my head to give me bunny ears. And Jessa was too busy giggling at all of us, her nose scrunched up and her hand raised to halfheartedly cover her mouth.

"You're all so cute," Cynthia mused as she admired the photo.

"Ugh, mom!" Wilder immediately went back into angsty teenager mode. 'Cute' wasn't an adjective she liked to hear.

Cynthia sent the photo to each of our parents, and they all printed it out at some point during our high school years. Personally, I know my parents printed the photo at Walgreens when Wilder was first diagnosed with neuroblastoma, and the doctors told her she had a 10% chance of survival. Hearing that destroyed me, so my parents thought having the photo around would somehow help. In the months following her diagnosis, I would stop every once in a while to look at the picture, which was framed and sitting on our mantle.

It was strange, seeing our smiling faces from less than a year before. We were all so much different by that point. Wilder's light brown hair had reached her shoulders that summer, and there were no dark circles encompassing her bright eyes. She was wearing a white My Chemical Romance shirt and black shorts. And I was in my cringeworthy 2011 look, dressed in a red Coca Cola graphic tee and cargo shorts, my hair a now-unimaginable length and swept to one side. Amari was in gym shorts and an American flag tank top, which he could actually get away with since he was on the junior varsity football team and wasn't a twig like me. He had let his hair grow out that summer, so the mini flat top he had for most of middle school was unruly. And Jessa had died her auburn hair jet black, which stood in stark contrast to the yellow sundress she was wearing in the photograph.

But after her diagnosis, Wilder shaved her head in anticipation of the inevitable hair loss chemo would cause. Amari and I got buzz cuts and Jessa cut her long hair to just above shoulder length, all in a sign of solidarity with our friend. We went from being innocent, babyfaced emo punks to dauntingly aware of mortality. We grew up fast, because Wilder was forced to face death. She had no choice in the matter. And we weren't about to let her face it alone.

For Wilder's memorial, her family had made collages with photos from her childhood. Among the dozens of pictures was the one from the barbecue. We were all gleefully gripping our cups, the contents a mystery to the rest of the world. Looking at the photograph, four years later, we went from being happy to being overwhelmingly grief-stricken. This summer day we weren't wearing t-shirts, shorts or sundresses, we were dressed in black suits and skirts. Our sneakers and flip flops had been replaced with shined shoes and flats. And our quick smiles had turned into tight-lipped grimaces.

Turning our attention from the photo boards, we went over to Wilder's family. We embraced each of them in a line. I was the last to go. Wilder's little sister, Lennon, hugged me first, her tears immediately staining my shirt. I couldn't think of anything to say, so I just let her cry as I stared at the wall, willing my eyes to stay dry. Lennon was twelve years old, and the spitting image of Wilder when she still had hair. Just less emo—that was Wilder's thing.

Next up was Crew. At fifteen, he didn't like hugs. He was gritting his teeth, and simply nodded when he saw me. If I didn't know him, I probably would have thought he was pissed at me. But it was just his way of coping.

"Take care of her," I whispered about Lennon. His eyes softened and he nodded again. When I walked away, he put his arm around his little sister, and soon his suit coat was drenched with her tears.

I shook Pete's hand, and he patted me on the back with a knowing look. He was a man of few words, and expected the same of everyone else.

It wasn't until I got to Cynthia that I finally started crying. She didn't even say anything to me, the floodgates just opened. She threw her arms around me and hugged me for what felt like an eternity.

"I'm so sorry," she sputtered.

"For what?" I asked in absolute disbelief. I should be saying sorry to her, she was the one who lost a daughter.

"I know how close you were," she explained, stepping back to look me in the eyes.

"Thank you," Cynthia went on. "You meant so much to Wilder."

"She meant a lot to me too," I whispered lamely, unable to keep the emotion from my voice.

"I hope your eulogy doesn't go like that," Amari muttered in my ear. I punched him in the kidney for saying that, but I appreciated his effort to keep it light.

The four of us moved to take our seats in the second row of the church, but first we had to pass by Wilder's casket. Her family had decided to keep it open. We hesitated for a moment before one of her aunts waved us over. Unsure of ourselves, we took three steps forward simultaneously. We held our breath like we were jumping into an ice cold lake, our eyes reluctantly peering into the casket.

The body laid out before us wasn't Wilder's. It didn't look anything like her. Her peach fuzz hair, which had started to grow back when she stopped treatments, was light brown against the white pillow her head was resting on. But that was as far as the similarities went. Her face was covered in make up the mortician had applied, and her hands, bruised from the lack of platelets in her blood, were clasped over her chest as opposed to flipping one of us off. And worst of all, she was wearing a *dress*. A white dress. Sleeveless.

"The fuck?" Amari said out loud. Jessa shushed him.

"I'm with him," Matt defended. "Wilder would be *pissed*."

"I know, but it's her parents' choice," Jessa whispered.

"I really would have thought they'd have gone with a David Bowie t-shirt," I said. "Or at the very least one of her polos."

"Right, she had some nice ass polos," Amari agreed. There was a pause as we all thought about Wilder's eccentric style.

Jessa giggled.

Matt snickered.

Amari grinned.

And somehow, on a day when I thought only tears were possible, I smiled.

five

My eulogy was like a leprechaun with a bad personality: short and terrible.

Try as we might, the four of us couldn't come up with words to adequately describe Wilder. So what I ended up saying, essentially, was that Wilder is the best person I've ever known, that she had an impact on everybody who knew her, and that my friends and I will miss her every day that we are alive on this earth without her.

My parents patted me on the shoulder and said that it was an eloquent tribute that showed how much Wilder meant to us; I felt as though it was cliche and oversimplified, two things Wilder was not. It wasn't the eulogy she deserved.

Her parents did a better job of encapsulating their daughter in a few words. It was tough to listen to, as neither of them were able to stop crying really. Their hope to make this a celebration of her life rather than a time to mourn her death had bellyflopped. It wasn't their fault; Wilder, as a person, made it extremely hard to say goodbye.

While we never really talked about her inevitable funeral, Wilder made it clear to me that she didn't want people to cry or be sad. I told her that was impossible—of course we were going to be sad when she was gone.

"Bitch," she had said with a massive eye roll. "Listen to me. If you're all sad and emotional about me being dead, then everything else will have been for nothing."

"What do you mean?" I asked as I dug my hand into a bowl of popcorn we had perched between us. It was four days after we got the news that she was dying. We were sitting on the couch in her living room, Wilder curled up in a ball under a throw blanket next to me. One of the Matrix movies was on the TV, but we had the volume muted so we could talk.

"Everything else," she said, her voice softer, less jaded. "Everything besides the cancer. All the memories. If you're sad you'll just be focusing on me being sick and eventually dead. But if you're happy, you'll be focusing on me."

There was a pause. I locked my eyes on the television and ignored the fact that all the oxygen in the room had just disappeared.

"And we all know how much I love being the center of attention," Wilder added. When I looked at her, she stuck her tongue out at me and giggled. Now it was my turn to roll my eyes.

"Okay," I ceded reluctantly.

"'Okay' as in you won't be sad?" she asked, sitting up a bit. I shrugged.

"I'll try my best," I replied. "But I can't guarantee anything." Wilder stared at me for a moment, contemplating if my answer was good enough. Finally, she nodded, distractedly scratching at her chest.

"Hey," I warned, throwing a piece of popcorn at her nose. At first she didn't know why I had done it, but then it clicked. Forty-eight hours earlier, she had undergone surgery to remove her port—the device that had been implanted when she was first diagnosed, then re-implanted when she relapsed, that the nurses used to draw blood and administer chemotherapy through. Since Wilder wasn't being treated anymore, the port was useless, and just prevented her from being able to swim. Fresh out of surgery, though, it was important she didn't scratch at it, or else the stitches could break.

We lapsed into silence, focusing on the moving pictures in front of us. I remember thinking how impossible her request was. Of course I was going to be sad. Of course her parents were going to cry. There wouldn't be a dry eye at her funeral. We were losing a remarkable individual.

And there was nothing we could do to stop it from happening.

*   *   *   *   *

I stood sandwiched between Amari and Matt in the front row of a large crowd of relatives and friends. We had already placed our roses on Wilder's closed coffin, right after her parents, siblings, and both sets of grandparents. Now, it was everyone else's turn.

I watched as teachers and classmates approached the coffin, their eyes downcast as they gripped their flowers carefully, avoiding the thorns on the stems. I saw Mrs. Holloway walk up with our chemistry teacher, Mr. Jaynes. They both nodded to us respectfully before returning to the crowd.

"Holy shit," Amari whispered to me, and I followed his gaze to see what he was talking about. Waiting in line to place his flower was Brady Pratt, one of Wilder's ex-boyfriends. He was the middle ex—not her first and not her most recent—but he was the most significant.

Brady was the punter on the high school's football team. He wasn't your stereotypical jock, though, which is why Wilder could justify dating him. He was quiet, with dark, sulking eyes that matched Wilder's slightly emo personality, but contradicted his light blonde hair. He wasn't a preppy douchebag that threw parties in his parents' mansion; he came from a working-class family and would sneak dollar beers from his parents' fridge to drink on Friday nights after his games.

It was the only time Wilder ever fell head-over-heels for a guy. Her first boyfriend was this goth kid named Isaac—he was a senior when we were sophomores—and he thought Wilder walked on water. Wilder, on the other hand, thought Isaac was just enough of a rebel to stay with him for five months. They broke up shortly after he graduated, with Wilder saying she didn't want a long-distance relationship when he went to college. Really, she had just gotten tired of him.

Brady was a different story. They started quietly dating shortly after she broke up with Isaac, and after two months, Wilder professed her love for him—which *really* wasn't like her. Don't get me wrong, Wilder was quick to say, "I love you" to pretty much everyone she cared about. But "love" meant something different in the context of Brady. She really had a thing for this kid. And when they broke up in February of this year, it hurt her. But she didn't admit it, at least not outright. However, she did get sourly drunk the following weekend.

After the break up, Brady and Wilder tried to stay friends. But like most couples that agree to do that, it didn't work out. Wilder was never at school once she relapsed, so she really had no reason to see him, and they just stopped texting. She never asked him to visit her in the hospital, and he never offered. Whenever Amari, Jessa and I would see him in the hall at school, he would look away and pretend we didn't exist.

And besides, both Brady and Wilder moved on. He started dating a cheerleader, Marissa Gates, and Wilder had a brief thing with this guy from South Burlington named Liam. Liam was the one who sprayed "I love you" on her wall.

Liam was lame. He didn't drink and only took a hit from Wilder's bong one time because everyone was on his ass for being a scrub. But he had a red Mustang, which was pretty nice to ride in. Regardless of his car, he wasn't rebellious enough for Wilder, and she dumped him. The way she talked about him, with a sort of faraway look in her eyes and a drag in her voice, made me think she regretted getting involved with him. But Wilder would never admit that herself. She was too proud.

Knowing Wilder's exes in detail helped me figure out who we would see at the funeral. Isaac was a no-show—he might not have even known Wilder had died—and I had spotted Liam with his mother in the back of the church earlier. He didn't speak to me, but he recognized me as one of kids that piled into the back of his Mustang. I genuinely did not expect Brady to show up at all; given that he had dropped off the radar after their break up, I figured he wouldn't feel obligated to attend.

After Brady placed his rose on the coffin, he strolled over to where we were standing, and while he pointedly nodded at each of us, he only extended his hand to me.

"I'm sorry," was all he said. I shook his hand and blinked, not sure of what to say in the situation. He didn't seem to notice; he just nodded again, more to himself this time, and turned away.

Brady melted into the crowd, returning to his role as a ghost in all of our lives.

six

Wilder had a thing for eyes. She couldn't draw faces well at all, except for eyes. All of her school notebooks had the margins filled with sketches of eyeballs, some more realistic than others. Whenever she was inpatient at the University of Vermont, the nurses would let her draw eyes on the windows with washable marker. From her room on the fourth-floor pediatric oncology unit, neon purple and green eyes gazed down at the courtyard garden, watching patients and visitors stroll through the rose bushes and infantile trees.

Wilder had captivating blue-green eyes. They were always alert, bright and constantly moving, scanning rooms and faces and the horizon for an indication of the future. I swear, Wilder could read minds. She could figure out what everyone was thinking just by looking into their eyes. But the same did not apply to Wilder—her eyes pulled you in, but they never gave anything away.

One time in art class, we had to draw portraits of people that inspired us. Most kids picked a celebrity, like Jimi Hendrix or Taylor

Swift, or a leader like the President or Gandhi. I picked Wilder, which sounds so cheesy when I say it out loud like this. It took me five weeks to finish the portrait, and even then, it still kind of sucked. But I got her eyes right.

"Dude!" Wilder exclaimed the day I gave it to her. "This is sick. Look at my eyes, they're perfect!"

I was visiting her in the hospital. It was a rainy May afternoon, shortly after Wilder relapsed. She had just had surgery to remove the tumors and was only a few days into her new chemotherapy regimen. She was sitting cross-legged on the bed, wearing her brother's faded football camp T-shirt and a pair of boxers she'd stolen from one of us. A pole with three bags hooked to it stood at attention next to the bed, tubes running from the plastic pouches to the port in Wilder's chest. One bag was filled with clear saline to keep Wilder hydrated. The other two bags were marked with frightening hazard symbols and bold warnings about the consequences of coming into contact with the contents. The liquids being pumped into Wilder's body—at that point it was ifosfamide and dinutuximab—were highly toxic. And yet, they were Wilder's only chance at living. It was a cruel irony that did not go unnoticed.

"What did you use for my eyes?" Wilder, a total art junkie, asked me. She didn't look up from the portrait, so she didn't notice my attention was focused on the tubes. Both drugs were misleadingly translucent. If it wasn't for the collage of hazard warnings, they could easily be mistaken for innocent saline.

"Just colored pencils," I mumbled. Wilder glanced up at me and grinned.

"This is awesome," she said. I smiled.

"I'm glad you like it,"

"I love it," she said just as one of her favorite nurses, Jana, walked in. Wilder held up the portrait, proudly proclaiming, "Look at what this loser did."

Jana set down her tray of medications and held the paper gingerly in her hands.

"Wow, this is spot on," she marveled. Then she shot me a look. "You did this, KJ?" I nodded.

Jana raised her eyebrows and nodded, seeming surprised that I had any sort of artistic ability.

"I think the eyes are my favorite part," she remarked. "You know what they remind me of? Lake Champlain during the Fourth of July lightning storm."

Wilder and I looked at each other and grinned. We knew what Jana was talking about —pretty much anyone who was at the waterfront in Burlington that day would have known.

The Independence Day Freak Storm, as the local high schoolers had come to call it, happened the year before. It had been a beautiful summer day, with an oppressively baby blue sky and not a single cloud in sight for miles. The pyrotechnicians who would be taking their boats out into Lake Champlain that night were excited to have such a clear sky to shoot their fireworks into. Around 2:00 in the afternoon, as kids and dogs ran around Waterfront Park and adults milled around drinking beer, a local band called Slum Fathers was setting up to play a free concert. Their backs to the water, the lead singer plugged in the last amp as he spoke into the microphone.

"Burlington," he called, feeling like Axl Rose. "Are you ready to light this park up?"

The plug clicked into place, and the sky suddenly flashed. Everyone saw it, but no one believed it. The singer paused, glancing at his bandmates to make sure they saw it too. A hush descended over the park, with everyone looking at the flawless sky for answers.

"Uh, that was—" the singer started to say "weird," but then another flash happened. And since now everyone was paying attention, they saw the jagged spike of electricity shoot through the sky.

A collective "whoa" rippled through the crowd. And then another bolt occurred, this one frightfully close to the busy park. The lightning struck the surface of Lake Champlain, emitting a loud *crack* that echoed throughout the waterfront. The little kids screamed and the parents rushed to get them as far away from the lake as possible. The teenagers, though, invincible in their adolescence, tip toed to the water's edge.

We were among those daring teenagers, stepping up to the low barriers that were meant to deter us from jumping into the lake. Wilder, Amari, Matt, Jessa, and I peered at the water, which seemed electrified, as if the lightning had altered its composition. It was a beautiful blue-green color, so clear that we could count the smooth pebbles that made up the shoreline.

Nurse Jana was right; Wilder's eyes in the portrait did match the electrified lake. Her eyes in real life bore more resemblance to a hurricane, though: they swirled with the ideals of a teenaged degenerate, the fears of a pediatric cancer patient, and the knowledge that a future isn't guaranteed to anyone, no matter how hard they fight for one.

Wilder's eyes never gave away what she was thinking, but they told her story better than words ever could. To look into her eyes was to enter her world: a world ravaged by a war that no child should ever have to fight.

*   *   *   *   *

In the weeks that followed Wilder's death, it felt like I was on some twisted roller coaster that I couldn't escape. For the most part, if I didn't think about the fact that a constant presence in my life had been violently ripped away from me, I was okay. But when my thoughts overpowered me, I turned into a mess.

I did my best to keep my tears to a minimum, because Wilder hated crying. She used to say, "There are two things no one looks good doing: running and crying." But some days I couldn't help it. Wilder was seventeen years old. She had her whole life ahead of her. She would have taken the world by storm, leaving an infallible mark on every person she came in contact with. And in a way, she had during her time here. But there was so much more for her. None of this was fair.

I spent a lot of time driving around the outskirts of Burlington, going up to Winooski or circling the Ethan Allen Homestead. Late one rainy afternoon, exactly three weeks after Wilder's death, I found myself in a parking lot in South Burlington. The lot was empty, and I was sitting in the driver's seat with the radio on. Thunder rumbled a few miles away, low and angry. The rain was coming down in sheets, pounding against my car. I turned the radio up so I could hear the next song over the downpour.

The first couple beats were familiar, but I didn't recognize which hip-hop track it was right away. I listened closely, my fingers tapping out the beat on the steering wheel.

"First thing's first, rest in peace Uncle Phil,"

I punched the power button.

Frantically, I searched my pockets, the console, the glove compartment—hell, even under my seat—for a pack of cigarettes. But I must've left them at home.

Something in me broke.

The only noise that filled my ears was the rain drowning my car and my own voice screaming as loud as it could.

The rest of J. Cole's "No Role Modelz" played out in my head, but it wasn't J. Cole rapping. It was Wilder's voice belting out the words as we kicked rocks down South Willard, a can of black cherry Four Loko in her hand. It was late, almost one in the morning, and it was just the two of us wandering the streets of Burlington together.

"C'mon," I slurred, my pink lemonade Four Loko halfway gone, just like myself. Loko always manages to fuck me up fast. "Enough with the J. Cole. Kendrick's way better."

"You shut your whore mouth," she exclaimed through bubbling laughter. I tried to focus my blurry eyes on her, the effort making it impossible to think of a comeback at the same time.

"I'm not wrong," I finally managed to say.

"Oh, here we go again," Wilder rolled her eyes. "I hung up on your ass the last time you said that." I raised the can to my lips. She was right: the first time I told her I thought Kendrick was better than J. Cole, she screeched into the phone and hung up. She called me back twenty minutes later, and said she had

62

found it in her heart to somehow forgive me, and we could continue to be friends. I grinned at the memory, which was foggy in my intoxicated mind. I lazily pointed my index finger in her direction.

"He's a *lyrical genie.*"

"A what?" she giggled. I stumbled forward, tripping over my own sneakers.

"Genius," I enunciated every letter. "I meant, *genius.*"

"Sure you did," she teased. "Maybe you should stop drinking that." I held the can out to her.

"And maybe you should—" I burped, the Loko not tasting nearly as good the second time around. "—mind ya own business."

"I'm just looking out for you," Wilder said. She looked at me skeptically and then added, "Hey, let's sit down."

"That's, that's a great idea," I agreed, aware of how pathetic I was but too drunk to feel bad about it.

We sat on the sidewalk of South Willard, street lamps keeping the darkness away from us. I held my can loosely in my hands, wondering what would happen if I drank all of it tonight. *I'd probably die,* I thought to myself.

"I really can't believe you think Kendrick Lamar is better than J. Cole," Wilder said after a few minutes. I snorted and put a hand to my face.

"Yeah, so what?" I asked, my eyes drooping.

"I just thought you were better than that." I snorted again, albeit delayed this time as I processed what Wilder said. More silence followed, and I closed my eyes, tired from spending the whole night walking around the town. We'd stopped at a mini mart two hours earlier and gotten our Lokos, purchased with the fake ID Matt had gotten me several months earlier. Thanks to my height and my habit of forgetting to shave on a regular basis, I could pass for a young twenty-one year old.

When I opened my eyes next, we were still on the sidewalk, but now Wilder was leaning against me, her head nestled in between my shoulder and neck. This wasn't unusual by any means; she laid on me constantly, because apparently I'm a better pillow than human.

She felt my head move and quietly asked, "KJ?" Her voice was small and soft, much less brash and certain than normal. I grunted in affirmation, unable to form words just yet. There was a pause, and for a moment I thought maybe Wilder didn't hear my grunt.

"Are you happy?"

The world started spinning around me, the trees and stores swaying in a booze-induced vortex. I stared at the pavement, forcing myself to think about Wilder's question.

"Right now?" I asked. The words were one, sloppy syllable.

"In general."

I thought some more. We'd gone swimming together earlier that day, for the first time in a long time. We'd spent the day laughing and pulling pranks and just being teenagers. I'd been content, nostalgic, grateful...but not happy.

I couldn't be happy because my best friend was dying. I couldn't be happy because there was no cure for cancer, even in 2015. I couldn't be happy because soon, my best friend would be in the ground and I would be lost. I would never be able to talk to Wilder again, hear her voice, hear her sing, see her laugh, just be in her presence.

I hadn't been happy since the day we found out she was dying. Happiness felt wrong. How could I justify being happy when Wilder's life was being cut short? There was no justice in her death. There was no rationale. She wasn't old and crippled. She was young, lively, full of passion and love. *She doesn't deserve this.*

"No,"

The word was ragged, husky and full of resentment for the circumstances. My answer was coupled with hot tears that streamed silently down my face. I set my can on the ground and quickly swatted them away, refusing to let Wilder see me emotional. She didn't seem to notice.

"Are you?" I asked, turning the question on her. She didn't answer for a long time.

"No,"

Wilder didn't want to die. There was so much she wanted to see and do and achieve. She wanted to go to college. She wanted to go on tour with a band. But she was forced to give all that up, to accept her fate and just *be okay with it*. No one's happy about dying, but they have to make their peace with death. They're expected to do that. Because if you don't make your peace with death, your family feels bad for the rest of their lives because there was nothing they could do to make you less scared and less pissed off that this was the hand you were dealt. And if Wilder had let on to that, had been honest with her family about how fucking terrified she was to die and how upset she was that there was *nothing she could do to change this*, her parents would have never been able to cope with her death. They would never be able to move on. And Wilder, in her selflessness, needed them to be able to move forward. For the sake of her siblings.

So she lied. She lied to her parents, to the social workers, to most of her friends. But when we were hammered that night at the end of June, she was honest with me. Because I was the one person she couldn't bullshit. Because I was the one person she trusted completely, and vice versa.

And I promised to never tell a single soul. I agreed to keep that knowledge, a solid burden that knotted my throat like a pair of headphones, locked in the recesses of my mind. It hung like a poster on the wall of my brain, announcing that Wilder Was Not Happy At The End Of Her Life And Was Destroyed By The Fact She Was Dying. Only I could see the poster, and it started driving me insane.

I peeled out of the parking lot I was in, still screaming without realizing it. I sped the entire way up Williston Road until I took a right hand turn going 30 miles per hour and screeched to a stop in the puddle-filled lot of a 7/11. My fists clenched around the steering wheel, I bent my head over the dash as my voice gave out and the tears that had filled my eyes the entire way here poured out onto the console.

"Fuck," I punched the steering wheel. "Fuck, fuck, *fuck*." I laid on the horn like a madman. I felt sick. I felt like I was going to explode. The back of my head buzzed.

I got my shit together, composed myself as best as I could, and got out of the car. I slammed the door shut, and walked into the 7/11 with no jacket. The door was only a few feet from my car, but the rain was coming down so hard I was drenched instantly. I stepped into the store, my sneakers splashing on the floor. The cashier glared at me.

"You the asshole doing all that honking?" I stared at him. He saw my face and immediately stopped glaring. Maybe it was the red splotches or the puffiness around my eyes, or how disheveled I looked in that moment. But it became evident from his body language that he felt bad for me for some reason.

I stumbled around the store and found what I was looking for. Bottle of water and a Snickers bar, a lighter—because if I didn't have a pack of cigarettes in my car, I probably didn't have a lighter, either—and the latest Alternative Press magazine.

I dropped everything on the counter and pulled out my debit card and fake ID. I tossed the ID on the glass as I asked for a pack of Marlboros. The cashier grabbed the red and white package from the wall behind him, but he kept glancing at me skeptically as he scanned my items. He picked up the ID and examined it for an uncomfortably long time.

I noticed his hesitation and looked up at him. He looked at the ID, then at me, then back at the card.

"Is there a problem?" I asked him, straightening my back. He shook his head.

"Nah, you just got a baby face," he mumbled.

"Yeah, I shaved this morning. Thanks for noticing."

Unamused, he slid my ID back across the counter and put my items in a bag. He told me halfheartedly to have a good day, and I stalked out of the 7/11 and back into the rain. I got in the car, which I had forgotten to lock in my haste to get cancer sticks.

With shaking hands, I broke open the pack and the lighter. I blew the smoke out of the cracked window, sideways falling raindrops taking advantage of the opening and landing on my lap. I sat in the parking lot for about twenty minutes before I flicked the cigarette butt to the asphalt and drove, slower and safer this time, back in the direction of Church Street.

seven

I drove to Wilder's house. I had been there several times since the memorial, mostly to help her parents out with repairs and projects, and to play video games or basketball with Crew. In the three weeks since Wilder had died, Crew had only spoken of his sister once—and that was because Cynthia had begged him, with tears in her eyes, to say something, anything. He, like his dad, didn't enjoy talking. But keeping things bottled up wasn't healthy.

If I could get Crew to talk about how he was handling Wilder's death, that would take a lot of pressure off Cynthia and Pete. That's why I spent so much time there still.

It stopped raining by the time I arrived at the Murray's house. I parked behind Pete's Mazda and walked around to the kitchen door, which I knew would be unlocked.

Showing up unannounced would normally be weird for other families, but Wilder's parents actually encouraged it. I walked into their kitchen and wiggled out of my shoes, announcing my presence by shouting, "It's KJ."

"Hi, KJ!" Cynthia called from a room upstairs. I heard footsteps coming down the hall, and Lennon poked her head around the corner.

"Hi," she said. She was a shy kid, completely opposite of Wilder. They got along, to an extent—Wilder protected her younger siblings, but she was a little disappointed that Lennon wasn't as outgoing and excited about life as she was. Cynthia and Pete didn't mind, though; of their three kids, Lennon would probably never smoke weed, and showed no inclination of getting drunk at one a.m. and wandering around the city unsupervised.

"Hey, Lemonhead," I said, using my nickname for her. I'd started calling her that when I was in middle school, and it stuck even after all these years. "Gotcha something." I opened the 7/11 bag and produced the Alternative Press magazine. Lennon's eyes lit up.

"For me?" she asked, eagerly taking the publication from my hands.

"All yours, kiddo," I sniffed at my shirt for the scent of smoke. Satisfied I didn't reek, I fished the Snickers bar out and stuffed the bag in a collection the Murrays had hanging on a cupboard door. "Crew home?"

"He's in his room playing Diablo," Lennon replied, her nose already buried in the magazine.

I ascended the stairs, walking down the hall to Crew's room. His door was shut, so I knocked twice.

"Ay man, it's KJ," I said.

"It's open," he called. I pushed the door in and found Crew sitting with his back against the headboard, his legs stretched out, button-smashing his PS3 controller.

"What's up," he greeted, not taking his eyes off the screen.

"Not much," I lied, not about to tell him that I was a complete wreck before driving over. "Here." I tossed the candy bar at him and it hit his torso. He glanced down at it briefly.

"Thanks," he muttered. If Wilder was an art junkie, Crew was a Snickers junkie and Lennon was a music junkie.

"Want to go to the rec center and shoot around for a bit?" I asked, sitting down on the edge of his bed. He contemplated the offer.

"Yeah, sure," he finally said, his voice devoid of any emotion. I smirked.

"Jesus, Crew, don't get too excited about it." He cracked a smile.

We left once he finished playing Diablo. About two minutes into our drive, Crew decided to start talking.

"Why are you still hanging around us?" he asked.

"What do you mean?"

"Wilder's dead," he said as if I didn't already know. "You were her friend. So why are you still hanging around my family? You feel bad for us or something?"

"Of course I feel bad for you guys," I said, a little amused at the absurdity of the conversation. "But I've been hanging around your family for the past six years. I'm not just going to walk away and pretend you guys don't exist because my friend died. I helped your parents out around the house before Wilder relapsed, and I'm not going to stop because she isn't here anymore."

Crew didn't say anything. When we came to a red light, I looked over at him. He was staring out the window as if he was trying to drill a hole in the glass.

"Do you not want me hanging out around your house?" I asked. He shook his head.

"It's not that," he said, his voice strained. He bit at his lips before running a hand over his head. "It's just, every time you come over, you're hanging out with me and Lennon or our parents. But like, you're supposed to be hanging out with Wilder. So it just makes her absence more pronounced."

The light turned green. I drove forward in silence for a bit, not sure exactly what to say.

"I get it," I finally replied lamely. "I'm sorry."

Crew shook his head again.

"It's fine," he said.

"It's not."

We pulled into the Burlington Recreation Center's parking lot, and Crew shot me a look.

"No, it's not," he muttered. "But it's just easier to say that it is."

We fell silent again, the car still running, each of us staring out the windshield.

"It's easier to tell people what they want to hear," I said. Crew nodded in agreement.

We shot around for a couple hours with a few twenty-somethings before I drove Crew home. We didn't talk about Wilder again.

"You staying for dinner?" he asked as he climbed out of the car. I shook my head.

"I've got plans," I said. "Maybe next week." He nodded and told me to have a good night. I waited until I saw the kitchen door shut behind him, and then headed home.

I didn't have plans. My parents and Meadow had already eaten by the time I got home, so I heated up a frozen pasta dinner and ate it in front of the TV. Dark circles had formed around my eyes from dehydration, but when I saw my reflection, I saw low platelet counts—something that Wilder dealt with constantly. The pasta that I had enjoyed countless times before tasted like sand in my mouth as I chewed robotically. I ended up throwing away half of it, partly because the taste was weird and partly because I didn't have much of an appetite. I walked nonchalantly past my parents and headed upstairs to change out of my gym clothes.

After I showered and got into a pair of pajamas, I started to settle in for the night. I had no intention of leaving my room until the morning. But then, Jessa called me.

"Hello?"

"KJ, hi," Jessa said. I could tell she had been crying from the way her voice was shaking. "What are you doing tonight?"

I glanced at the clock. It was almost 10 p.m. on a Monday night.

"Nothing, why?"

"Do you mind picking me up?" she asked. "If not it's okay."

"Where are you?" I asked, starting to pull on a hoodie. "Is everything okay?"

"Yeah," she said. Then, "No. My stepdad... he's out of control again."

"Are you safe?"

"Yeah, I'm waiting outside the house right now," Jessa replied. "But I think it might start raining soon."

"I'll be there in ten," I said.

I headed downstairs and grabbed my keys from the counter.

"Where are you heading in your pajamas?" my mom asked from the family room.

"Jessa needs a ride," I answered, halfway honest.

"A ride to where?"

"Dunno." They didn't know about Jessa's home life. And frankly, if they did, they would tell me not to involve myself. But Jessa was my friend. I wasn't going to leave her hanging.

I left in the midst of my parents' protests, hopping in and starting my car before they had a chance to stop me. I got to Jessa's house, on the same street as Wilder's, and found her waiting for me by the mailbox. She climbed in the passenger seat and happily picked up the pack of Marlboros.

"Where do you want to go?" I asked, ready to be the chauffeur for the night.

"Anywhere," she said, lighting the cigarette as she held it between her teeth. "Just drive."

eight

In fifteen minutes, I had gotten us to Thayer Beach in Colchester. Thayer Beach is situated in Malletts Bay, which looks out at Vermont's Grand Isle to the north, and the state of New York to the west. Although, you really can't see either, given the distance; but you know they're there.

Jessa and I didn't speak the entire time we drove north. She spent the car ride staring out the window at the sparsely lit roadside. It started to rain when we got to the Winooski River bridge, offering some distraction from the silence that sat between us.

I knew Jessa's stepdad, David Lambert, was a cocky electrician who had been out on disability for the past two years. He had a short temper and threw things when he got angry. And more often than not he was angry, because all day he just sat around in his La-Z-Boy drinking Switchback and watching Fox News. Beer preference and means of supply were the only good things about David; he always had at least two cases of Switchback in the basement fridge, which made it easy for us to sneak bottles unnoticed when he was in the bathroom.

Jessa's mom, Karen, had been with David for the better part of four years. When they got married, Jessa's two older sisters made it very clear that they wanted to get out of the house as soon as possible. None of them liked David, and her sisters, Samantha and Whitney, wanted to go to New York to live with their dad.

But Mr. O'Connor, who I had never met, wasn't much better than David. From what I could gather, O'Connor was a deadbeat living in Saratoga Springs, where he spent all his money betting on horses. Samantha went to school down in Albany and tried to convince him to let her and Whitney move in with him. But he refused. He didn't want to have to support them anymore than he already had—after all, by that point, Samantha was eighteen and Whitney was sixteen. He was almost down to just one child support payment. Why should he take on more financial burden?

In the present day, Samantha was twenty-two, fresh out of college, and Whitney was twenty. Both still lived at home, with Karen—who worked two jobs to pay the bills—and David, an explosive alcoholic. Daily shouting matches had become routine at Jessa's house.

She did everything she could to stay away from it all. And when Wilder was alive, that was pretty easy.

Jessa would stay at Wilder's on the nights when David flew off the handle. But since the memorial, Jessa hadn't gone to Wilder's house. No matter how bad things got with David, Jessa couldn't bring herself to spend the night at the Murray residence. Not without Wilder there.

I couldn't really blame her. Admittedly, it was weird to be at the house without Wilder. For as close as I was with her parents and siblings, I still felt like an outsider without her to start conversations. And for as much as I was hurting, I felt like an outsider to their grief. They were her flesh and blood. I was just a close friend.

As I thought about it, I realized I wasn't entirely sure why Wilder and Jessa were even friends. They were so different from each other. I guess they were similar to me and Amari: they grew up on the same street, so by default a friendship formed.

Wilder and Jessa balanced each other out. Wilder was spontaneous and impulsive, while Jessa was responsible and thoughtful. Jessa kept Wilder grounded, and Wilder helped Jessa dream a little bigger. Wilder kept to herself as Jessa ran for class president and won the title of Prom Queen. They didn't seem like they would be as close as they were. And maybe they wouldn't have if Jessa didn't live up the street with a raging alcoholic.

I parked the car in Thayer Beach, the engine pointing north towards the shadowy Grand Isle. We listened to the *pitter-patter* of the rain mix with the slow rolling tide of the lake. It was relaxing, and I took what felt like my first real breath of the day.

Sleep started to overtake me. I felt my eyelids drooping, but I willed myself to stay awake. I looked over at Jessa, who had the side of her head resting against the window.

"You okay?" I asked. She shrugged.

"It's just a lot," she whispered.

"That's for sure," I agreed. "You don't need to deal with David's bullshit right now."

"I keep telling my mom to leave him, but she says we don't have the money for a divorce lawyer," Jessa shook her head. "But really, I think she just doesn't want to leave him. She's afraid he won't be able to support himself, and she feels obligated to take care of his lazy ass."

"He's getting disability checks, he can take care of himself. He would just have to stop buying so much beer." Jessa smirked.

"Yeah, but we all know that'll never happen."

A few minutes went by before Jessa spoke again.

"I miss Wilder."

"Me too." She looked up at me, and even in the darkness I could see the tears welling in her eyes.

"I want her back so bad."

The words were barely audible. I reached over and put my arm around her as best as I could in the car, my own eyes starting to burn with tears.

"Come on," I said, trying to be the "strong" one. "Wilder wouldn't want us to be blubbering messes. She wasn't about that."

"I don't care," Jessa sobbed into my hoodie. "I just want her back."

There wasn't anything that I could say or do to make this better. There wasn't some magic remedy, a string of words that would erase the pain. Because when your best friend dies, there is nothing to say.

If I told Jessa, "She's in a better place," I would have gotten smacked. Because even if heaven exists, Wilder didn't want to be in a better place. She wanted to be here on Earth, with its morons and natural wonders and disasters and pain because at least then she would be with the people she cared about, laughing and dancing and loving and living.

If I told Jessa, "She's not in pain anymore," I would have gotten an eye roll. Because yes, Wilder suffered a great deal. Of course she did. She had cancer. She was pumped full of toxic chemicals six times a week. She had nasty scars from surgery. She was lethargic, nauseous, sore. But she was *alive*. Wilder herself once said, "I wold rather be going through all this and alive, than be pain-free and dead."

If I told Jessa, "Everything happens for a reason," I would probably be at the bottom of Lake Champlain. There was no reason for Wilder to get sick and die. There is no Greater Meaning to her death. The universe or God or fate decided that, You know what? Wilder Sage Murray doesn't get to live. She doesn't get to grow up or even see her eighteenth birthday. She gets to be one of the greatest humans to ever walk on this oversized rock, but only for seventeen years, six months and fifteen days. And then she'll die, and leave a giant, scathing hole in all these people's lives. And they'll never be the same, they'll never smile the same way, because the jokes she used to tell will never be delivered right by anyone else.

So that left us with one question.

When words fail, what do you do?

*   *   *   *   *

Jessa didn't want to go home. She was an emotional wreck, and according to a text from her sister Whitney, David was still raging. By the time we finished talking at Thayer Beach, it was 12:45 a.m. I couldn't pull an all nighter since I had work at noon. Having known Jessa for six years, I offered to let her spend the night at my place.

"Are your parents going to be okay with that?" she asked skeptically. I shrugged.

"I'm helping a friend out. If they get pissed at me for that, screw 'em."

The front door of my house was unlocked, something my mom always made a point of doing whenever I was out late. Jessa and I took off our sneakers in the front hall and carried them up the stairs, careful to step in unison. We hurried past my parents' room at the top of the landing, and moved even faster past Meadow's room. I knew my parents were most likely asleep, but Meadow stayed up till two in the morning usually, scrolling through Tumblr.

Luckily for us, no one stirred.

I shut the door to my room before clicking on the light. I tossed Jessa one of my undershirts and a pair of gym shorts and dutifully waited with my back turned. We split the bed in half, with Jessa curling up by the headboard and me laying with my legs dangling off the edge of the bed.

Jessa passed out pretty quickly, but for as exhausted as I was, I couldn't seem to fall asleep. I thought about when Wilder used to spend the night at my place. It wasn't often, but there were a few Friday nights, back when she was NED, when my parents would let her sleep over.

Most of the time, we'd set up blankets on the couches in the family room and sleep down there while infomercials played on the TV. But one night we had been up repainting the walls of my bedroom, and that's how I knew to split the bed in half with Jessa.

It was the weekend before Mother's Day 2014. Wilder and I had spent most of that Saturday painting my room blue, as opposed to the off-white it had been for the past seven years. She was on the maintenance chemo, so her hair had grown back a little bit. It was still short and fuzzy, which she actually enjoyed because people rubbed her head often to feel it. My mom wanted us to paint the room in clothes that we wouldn't care about getting dirty, so we were dressed the same: white Hanes undershirts and old gym shorts.

We got them from the bottom of my dresser. The undershirt fit me normally, but it was about three sizes too big on Wilder's petite frame. The shorts, which were red and gold and from my cringe-y middle school days, were too loose for her, so she pulled the drawstring to tighten them. But she had to pull the string so far that it hit the floor.

"God damn it, KJ," she feigned with a giggle. "I thought you were a runt in middle school?"

"I thought so too," I said earnestly.

"I guess I'm smaller than a thirteen year old boy," she had muttered, and we both laughed.

We finished painting my room around midnight, and once we had cleaned up, we flopped onto my bed in exhaustion. We had only meant to take a couple minutes to scroll through Instagram and Twitter, but we both ended up falling asleep. I woke up at two a.m. with Wilder's foot in my trachea, which isn't exactly the most comfortable thing in the world. I pushed her away from me, towards the headboard, and that solved the problem pretty easily.

A year later, when Wilder was inpatient after her relapse, I stayed late at the hospital. Normally only family members get to spend the night, but every nurse in the pediatric oncology unit knew that Wilder and I were pretty much siblings. They offered to bring in a cot for me to sleep on, but we had our half-bed system figured out. The lights were turned off in the room, and we settled down in our respective halves. I was almost asleep when Wilder's voice startled me awake.

"You up?"

"Yeah," I said once my heart stopped pounding.

"Can I ask you something?"

"You just did,"

"Fuck you," I could hear Wilder's eyes roll, and I smiled.

"Sorry," I laughed. "Go for it, ask me." There was a pause.

"Do you believe in heaven?"

If Wilder hadn't just relapsed, I would have been appalled she asked me such a question— she hated talking about religion. But I knew death was weighing heavily on her mind, since her chances of survival had dropped to about 1%.

"I believe in something," I responded carefully. "I don't know what, exactly. But I don't think we just die and that's it, everything goes black and—game over. I do think there's something after this."

Another pause.

"Like reincarnation?"

"Maybe," I said. "Or maybe we just become ether. I really don't know."

"You don't know, but you believe in something regardless?"

"Well, yeah," I shifted uncomfortably at my end of the bed. "I kind of have to."

"Why?"

"I guess just 'cause I was raised Catholic, I was raised to believe in an afterlife. So there's that, but also…if there's nothing waiting for us when we die, then what's the point of all of this?"

"Maybe there is no point," Wilder said. "Maybe it's just a cruel game, and like you said, we just die and that's it. Just blackness."

"There's gotta be something more," I argued. "Something better."

More silence followed.

I closed my eyes again, but made sure I stayed awake.

"Do you believe in angels?"

"Yes," I said with my eyes still closed.

"Why?" I paused as I tried to formulate a strong thesis.

"I believe that when people die, they're still around," I finally replied. "Like, right after my uncle died, my grandpa got in a car accident. And these electrical wires fell on his car, all exposed and stuff, and they should have electrocuted the car and him. But they didn't. And a tow truck just happened to be driving down this deserted road where it happened, and the dude stopped and helped my grandpa get out of the car.

"He didn't have a scratch on him. He and the driver didn't get electrocuted, when they really should have. No one could explain it. When the cop showed up, all he said was, 'Wow, sir, you must have somebody looking out for you up there.' And my grandpa was sure it was my uncle."

"So you believe in angels because there's miracles to prove they exist?" Wilder asked. My eyes opened. I thought about how I knew there were exposed pipes painted eggshell white crossing the ceiling above me, even if I couldn't see them in the darkness.

"Not necessarily because of miracles," I answered. "But because I...I need it to be true."

I thought about how badly I would need angels to be real if Wilder died. I needed her to still be around, somehow, watching out for me like she did when she was alive. My cheeks burned at the notion of Wilder not being around. I refused to believe she wouldn't go into remission again.

I wanted to say something just so Wilder's voice would push the silence out of the room. I wanted to know she was still there, at the other end of the bed. But when I opened my mouth to speak, no sound came out. I figured by the time I stopped choking on my words, she would be asleep.

But she couldn't fall asleep, because she posed another question:

"What about hell?"

"You're not gonna go to hell, Wilder."

"I didn't say I was gonna die, asshole."

"Well that's what this is about, isn't it?" I asked, propping myself up on my elbows. Wilder sat up, pulling her knees to her chest. "You're asking about all of this because you're scared."

"I'm not scared," she snarled.

"It's okay to be scared," I said gently. "You have every right to be."

"I'm not though,"

"Wilder,"

"What?"

"Stop bullshitting."

Another pause, followed by a sigh.

"Yeah, I'm scared, KJ. You know what a 1% chance of survival feels like? A death sentence."

"You felt that way about the 10% chance back when you were first diagnosed."

"This is different," Wilder's tone softened. "I cheated death once already. I don't know if I can pull it off again."

"You will," I reassured her. "You're the reigning champ over death." She grinned.

"Heavyweight or lightweight?"

"Oh, lightweight, for sure," I scoffed. "Are you kidding? You're ninety pounds soaking wet."

"I'm a lightweight that drinks like a heavyweight," she added.

"That's accurate," I snickered. "You tolerate alcohol better than me."

"It's the luck o' the Irish."

The luck o' the Irish. I could still hear her say that, in her best Irish accent. I cringed remembering what I said about Wilder being the reigning champ. Had I jinxed it? Did I believe in jinxes? Or was it already predestined?

Had Wilder always been meant to die so young?

nine

The next morning, my parents left for work and took Meadow to summer camp. Once I heard their car pull away, Jessa and I got up and got dressed. We went to Dunkin Donuts for breakfast and coffee, and then I dropped her off at her house.

"Thanks for letting me crash at your place," she said before she got out of the car. "I really appreciate it."

"Of course," I said. "Hopefully things work out with your mom."

I drove back home and showered, got ready for work, and texted Amari to see if he wanted a ride to Church Street since I was going over there anyway. He took me up on the offer, and around eleven we climbed into Gordy and drove over to the marketplace.

The rain from yesterday seemed like a faraway memory. The sky was bright blue, with fluffy white clouds that bore no threat of storms. I told Amari about what happened with Jessa, and he said he would head over to see her later. But first, could he borrow my basketball?

"I might meet Matt to shoot around on the outdoor courts at UVM," he explained.

"It's in the backseat," I said.

"Sweet," Amari reached into the back and grabbed the Spalding.

"How's Matt doing, anyway? I haven't seen him in a while."

"He's alright. He and Emily are broken up for good it seems, so he's bummed about that. He's kind of holed himself up in his apartment," Amari answered. After the memorial, our group chat faded because we felt weird texting it, since it still had Wilder's number included, and Matt had all but dropped off the radar. He texted Amari occasionally, but their conversations never lasted long.

As for Jessa and I, we weren't very close with Matt. I think that's why it was so easy to let him drift away and not think twice about it. He was closer with Wilder than he was with the rest of us. Matt thought she was the funniest person he'd ever met. Wilder was drawn to his confidence, which was mostly built by a harmless arrogance that he was blind to. The two of them bonded over painting; the only thing I had in common with him was the need for a fake ID.

When we all hung out together, he always struck me as a little pretentious, subtly judging everyone except Wilder. He would stay quiet for the most part, unless he was laughing at something Wilder did or said. He was angsty, a starving, tortured artist who personified the term 'brooding.' In comparison to Amari, Jessa, and I, Matt was too serious. Maybe that's why Wilder liked having him around. Perhaps he was a warning of what the rest of us could become if we took life too seriously.

According to his on-again-off-again girlfriend, Emily, Matt had an addictive personality. When he grew more distant, I wondered briefly if he was drinking himself numb to cope with Wilder's death. I knew I felt like doing the same thing. But I resisted, because Wilder would call it the loser's way of dealing with shit. I wondered if Matt knew that too, or if he hadn't really listened to her when she spoke. If he was too wrapped up in his own angst to recognize Wilder was teaching him something. Teaching us all something.

"You know he's vaping now?" Amari's voice suddenly broke through my thoughts.

"Matt did not start vaping," I said in disbelief.

"Oh, he did," Amari grinned like the Cheshire Cat. "He's a real vape connoisseur now."

"Oh come *on*," I groaned. "Vape bitches are so lame."

"I told him that, but he didn't seem to care. He said smoking is his way of coping, but he doesn't want to smoke cigarettes anymore because of the whole cancer thing."

"No one knows what they put in vape. They could cause cancer just as much," I muttered. I pulled into the lot behind Burton and we got out, deciding to walk up to Starbucks. Amari wanted to get something to drink before he went to UVM, and I needed something to do before my shift started. I didn't want to be sitting in the car alone with my thoughts again. There were no 7/11's around here.

"Man, it's gonna suck going back to school," Amari said as we sat down to wait for his drink. He kept the basketball corralled in between his feet as he scrolled through his Instagram feed. I hadn't even thought about the approaching school year. I didn't want to. I knew that things would be different, not because Wilder wouldn't be there—she was hardly at school when she was alive, given her compromised immune system—but because our teachers would see us as broken for the first couple of months. And then they would forget. Just like our classmates would forget, until it was time to graduate, and the valedictorian would say a little dedication to honor the fallen member of our class year.

"And we have to start applying to colleges soon, too," Amari continued absentmindedly. "I'm trying to get recruited to Rutgers."

"Rutgers?" I said, not really paying attention.

"Yeah, I talked to the coach there and he said I might have a shot at getting on the team, if I do well at the combine next week."

"Combine?"

"Yeah, there's that combine down in New Jersey. Coaches from like, six different schools are gonna be there."

"You're going?" I asked. This was the first time I had heard anything about Amari traveling out of state.

"Yeah man, I told you like, last week," he stared at me briefly, then shook his head. "You were high as a kite though, so maybe you don't remember."

I racked my brain trying to figure out when Amari had told me about the combine and Rutgers. We had gone to UVM to get high twice last week, so it must have happened sometime around then.

"Sorry," I mumbled. Amari shrugged.

"It's all good," he said, putting his phone down. "How you doing, man? You holding up?"

"Not really," I answered. "Everything reminds me of Wilder, and I feel like I'm drowning constantly. All I wanna do is scream." He looked at me thoughtfully. I knew what was going on in his head. Feeling guilty, I looked out the window, watching people roam around the marketplace.

Before I met Wilder in sixth grade, Amari had been my closest friend. I was shy and he was an only child, which led to us coming to the realization that we needed each other. An arguably codependent bond was formed, which was only augmented by us being neighbors. We hung out after school together, eating pizza rolls and doing homework. We were on the same flag football team for a couple seasons before I decided I was better off in band. And then we got to middle school, and Wilder entered the scene.

Amari and Wilder butted heads at first, for reasons unknown to me back then. When we got older and more mature—and high—Amari admitted to me that he had felt threatened by Wilder. He didn't want to be replaced as my best friend by some random girl.

Wilder, unlike me, knew from the beginning why Amari didn't get along with her. She made every effort to appease him, being sure to include him in pretty much everything we did. That's why he's always been a part of our core group: Wilder didn't want to deliberately tear apart our friendship.

But there's no denying that Wilder acted as a wedge between us, even if she didn't mean to. She became my confidant, not Amari. She was the person I talked to the most. I spent more time at her house rather than Amari's. But to his credit, if he ever felt jealous, he didn't really let on to it—especially when she was diagnosed with cancer. If she hadn't been sick, if the threat of death didn't loom above her, maybe things would have been different. Priorities wouldn't have gotten sorted. Maybe our friend group would have experienced typical high school pettiness. But we didn't have the privilege of being typical.

When Wilder died, the wedge she inadvertently drove between me and Amari didn't quite disappear. In a sense it did, because we spent more time together now that she was gone. But our relationship wasn't like a rubber band; we didn't just snap back to the way we were pre-Wilder. There was this unnamed tension between us, because we both knew there were things we couldn't say to each other. Amari knew I couldn't talk to him like I talked to Wilder, and he could never tell me how let down he felt by my friendship with her because it paled in comparison to her death.

So we pretended. We put on invisible masks when we were around each other, masks of lighthearted smiles that made it seem like we were closer than before. We talked about Wilder, and how much we missed her. But the tension was always there. The knowledge that the other was holding back, not being completely honest, kept us from being our true selves.

I swallowed, wondering if I should acknowledge the tension. I started to say something, but someone interrupted me.

"Hey, Amari, KJ." We looked up. It was Brady Pratt, dressed in a blue and white button up, chino shorts and Sperry's. Amari glanced at his shoes, then looked at me with raised eyebrows. I knew what he was thinking. *Wilder would throw a fit if she saw how preppy he looks.*

"What's up, Brady?" Amari asked.

"You going to the combine down in Atlantic City next week?"

"Yeah, are you?"

"I want to, but coach wants me practicing here. He says I'll probably get recruited when the scouts come to our regular season games." Amari narrowed his eyes but didn't say anything. Brady turned to me.

"KJ, I was wondering if I could talk to you about something,"

"Sure," I said. But Brady didn't speak. His eyes fluttered between me and Amari for a few moments. Finally, Amari got the hint.

"Y'know what, I'm gonna head up and find Matt. I'll see you later." He scooped up the basketball and took his drink from the counter and left. Brady sat down in his empty seat. As Amari strolled past the window, he rolled his eyes at me in exasperation. I covered my mouth to hide my smirk and watched as Brady nervously twiddled his thumbs.

"What's going on?" I asked him. He stared out at the marketplace as he slowly formed his sentence.

"I know you were really close with Wilder," he began, and I sat up straight in my seat, not sure where this was going. "And I know you two talked about me. About us."

"No, never," I said with massive sarcasm. Brady's mouth twitched with a half smile.

"I've always felt bad about the way things ended," he continued. "And how I kind of dropped the ball on staying friends with her. Especially...at the end." His inflection of that last part made it sound more like a question rather than a statement.

I stared at him blankly.

"Wilder didn't really go around telling people she was dying," I explained. "You didn't know so you couldn't have done anything to make up for lost time." Brady glanced down at the table.

"The thing is, though, I did know."

He raised his eyes to me.

"She texted me back in June. She said she was going into hospice care, and that was it. She left it open ended, I think so I didn't feel obligated to go see her."

"Which you didn't," I said, a bitter taste in my mouth. Wilder never told me she had reached out to Brady. The fact that she had, and he never went to see her—especially given how she had felt about him—made me want to smash his face into the table.

Brady could sense my growing resentment. He sat back in his chair and blinked as he looked out the window.

"I feel awful," he said, his voice constrained by emotion. I glared at the floor, my teeth clenched together to keep me from screaming.

"I should have gone to see her."

A single tear fell to his lap.

"She loved you,"

The words were almost inaudible in the coffee shop. But Brady heard them, his head snapping to attention.

"What?" His eyes were wide as he searched my face for proof that I was lying. My glare switched from the floor to him.

"She loved you," I repeated each word deliberately, my voice still low. Brady's mouth formed an "o" shape, and he seemed genuinely surprised. I shook my head.

"She hated most jocks. You and Amari are pretty much the only exceptions. I don't know what she saw in you, but I know it wasn't that." I nodded at his Sperry's. Brady gazed at his shoes as if he could see Wilder's disappointed face in them.

"You were the only guy she dated that she actually, truly, cared about," I was on a roll now. "She said 'I love you' first because she meant it."

I felt the tears creeping up on me. I looked at the time on my phone. My shift was starting soon.

I stood up.

"She loved you," I said again. "And you fucking abandoned her."

ten

Brady was on the verge of tears as he followed me into the Burton store. He was trying to talk to me, and it was evident I was ignoring him. Travis, the co-worker I got into the car accident with, and my manager Andrea were working when we walked in. Brady was a frenzy of emotions. I was stone cold and expressionless.

"KJ, you have to understand," he was saying. "I thought if I went to see her I'd just cause her more pain."

"Oh, fuck off," I muttered under my breath so the customers wouldn't hear. I turned to face him. "That's such a cop out. You know Wilder. You know how strong she is. She's had cancer twice, you really think you're *that* significant by comparison?"

There was silence in the store. I realized I was talking about her in the present tense. Brady took a step back.

"You're right, KJ," he said, holding up his hands. "You are absolutely right. I guess I'm just an asshole."

"What, did you want me to make you feel better?" I scoffed. "Did you really show up today to tell me your sob story and expect me to say, 'Oh, Brady, it's alright, I'm sure Wilder would have forgiven you.'"

Brady stared at the ceiling. I started laughing bitterly.

"Yeah, you're an asshole for not going to see her. You didn't have an excuse not to at least stop by to say hi. To let her know you *cared* about her. You got a text saying, 'I'm dying,' and you didn't even bother to send a text back?" My voice was starting to rise, and the customers stopped shopping to watch the scene unfold in front of them.

"Wilder deserved better than what she got. And I don't just mean cancer." Brady looked at me, his mouth dropping in anticipation of what I was going to say next.

"She deserved better than you."

Stark silence descended over the store.

"She treated you like gold," I spat, my voice low and gravely. "Even after the breakup. She never once talked badly about you. Yet you turned your back on her."

Brady and I were locked in a staring contest.

"We don't do that sort of thing," I whispered. "We don't turn our backs on the ones we care about."

Someone in the store let out a little cough.

"So yeah, Brady," my voice was almost inaudible again. It shook with emotion. "You're an asshole. It's really too bad Wilder didn't see that when she was alive."

Brady nodded, biting his lower lip. He looked around, saw everyone watching us, and spun on his heels. He left the store, leaving me feeling drained but a little victorious.

Now that he was gone, everyone's attention was on me. I looked over at Andrea. She was staring at me as if she'd never seen me before in her life.

"Sorry about that," I said, starting to fold shirts by the center display. There was a few seconds of delay before things went back to business as usual. Neither Andrea or Travis brought up the incident with Brady. I worked the first half of my shift in almost complete silence, only talking when I had to. Around four, I took my lunch when Nate came in for the shift change.

I sat on the hood of my car, eating a granola bar and watching the traffic pass by. Travis, who was being replaced by Nate, came out of the store room and sauntered over to my car, his head bobbing up and down as he walked.

He climbed up onto the hood next to me and leaned forward, his arms resting on his knees.

"Who was the guy earlier?" he asked, squinting in the sunlight.

"Wilder's ex-boyfriend,"

"Really?" Travis raised his eyebrows at me. "He didn't really seem like her type."

"He wasn't a preppy fuckboy when she knew him," I said. Travis nodded.

"Makes more sense,"

I finished my granola bar and stuffed the empty wrapper in my pocket. I glanced at Travis uneasily.

"How come you're still here?" I asked. He laughed and swung his arm over my shoulder.

"What, I can't hang out with my homie on his break?" I pushed him off.

"You just finished a seven hour shift," I told him. "What's the deal?" He sighed and scratched the back of his head.

"Andrea's worried about you, asked me to check in on you." I looked back at the store thoughtfully.

"Yeah, I'm fine," I said. Travis nodded, taking what I said at face value.

"Cool," he hopped off the hood of the car, his task done. "Let me know if you need anything."

I thanked him and watched as he got into his new car—it was a 2004 Acura RSX with 100,000 miles on it, but it was new compared to the car that got totaled back in January.

I remembered the cold, sudden fear that had greeted me when I woke up in the hospital after the accident. It was a fear that rose above the pain medication once my consciousness realized I was in a foreign place, unable to move my body freely. My heart pounded as I scrambled for answers in that bright, sterilized room. But the fear subsided once I saw my parents, and they explained where I was and what happened. And that I was okay.

I watched the Acura turn left out of the parking lot. That feeling of fear was something I would never be able to forget. And I felt it now, for whatever reason. My heart pounding so hard it was close to exploding out of my chest; my eyes darting rapidly, searching for answers to unasked questions. I felt like I might die.

Was this how Wilder felt at the end?

Was she panicking?

Did she feel an unconscious fear that rose above the high dose of morphine?

I laid back against the windshield, my arms crossed over my face. I laid like that until the alarm on my phone went off, signaling the end of my lunch break. I slid off the hood, pushing my thoughts of Wilder out of my head. I had to finish my shift.

*   *   *   *   *

Around 6:30, the store was empty. Most marketplace goers were at dinner, not shopping for Burton merchandise. Andrea had gone home for the day, so it was just me and Nate running the place.

We kept the door open to entice whatever wanderers passed by, which meant the bell didn't ring when they walked in since it didn't sense the door opening and closing. Nate and I were standing behind the counter, packaging up online orders and talking shit, so we didn't notice a customer slip in.

It wasn't until Nate went to get a product from the shelf that he saw the customer. He eyed him nervously and came back to the counter empty-handed.

"What's Andrea's policy on kids again?" he asked me. I didn't look up from the box I was packing.

"Under ten they have to be with an adult," I murmured.

"How old d'you think that kid is?" Nate asked, nodding with his head. I glanced up. There was a little boy standing by the shoe display, admiring the boots. I shrugged.

"Seven, eight maybe,"

Nate looked at the boy, then at me. He raised his eyebrows pointedly.

"Well?"

"Well what?" I asked. He rolled his eyes.

"You gonna kick him out?" I smirked.

"Bruh, he's not doing anything wrong,"

"Store policy," Nate sang as he walked into the back room.

"Fill your damn order," I called after him. The kid looked up at me. I said, "Your parents with you?" He shook his head.

"They sent me in here while they buy my birthday presents," he explained. His voice was high pitched, but he was articulate.

"Don't break anything," I warned, and turned my attention back to the order.

The boy watched me for a moment, then came up to the counter. He watched me fill the box and stayed quiet.

"Can I help you?" I muttered without looking up. He tilted his head to one side.

"How old are you?"

"Seventeen," I answered. The boy didn't say anything to that. Nate came out of inventory carrying merchandise for the order.

"Is he your boss?" I looked at Nate and grinned.

"He wishes," I replied. Nate scowled.

"I've been here longer than you, that makes me superior."

"Not if I'm better at my job," I countered. "Andrea trusts me more than you, anyway."

"Oh, bull—" Nate stopped himself and eyed the little boy. He was watching us, absorbing everything.

"What was that?" I taunted him. Nate took my order from me.

"Why don't you give the kid some stickers, huh?" The boy smiled up at me and nodded slightly, encouraging me.

We kept a basket of stickers under the counter for the little kids that came in the store sometimes, and for the customers that wanted decals for their boards or laptop covers. I brought the basket up and pushed it towards the boy. He stood on his tip-toes and peered at the variety eagerly.

"Take as many as you want," I told him, knowing we had a surplus. The stickers only cost fifteen cents wholesale, and we had reams of them in the back room. If ever there was an apocalypse and stickers were the only key to survival, we could save all of Vermont and probably New Hampshire.

The kid dug around in the basket for a little bit and eventually settled on five stickers of different sizes and shapes, but all of which branded Burton in one way or another. He peeled one of the stickers off of its paper backing and stuck it to his shirt. He shoved the rest in his pocket.

"Do you snowboard?" he asked me. I nodded. Wilder and I used to snowboard down at Killington Resort when she wasn't too sick. She introduced me to the 3,050 foot vertical drop, turning me into a halfway adrenaline junkie. I grinned at the memory of my first time going down the drop. I almost shit my snow pants.

The kid kept going, "Is that why you work here?"

"I guess," I said. "Do you snowboard?" The boy nodded proudly, puffing out his chest.

"I'm gonna be in the X Games when I'm older."

"Yeah?" Nate said, the bold statement piquing his interest. He rested his arms on the counter. "What makes you say that?"

"My cousin was in the X Games in January," the boy explained. "She says I'm gonna be just as good as her when I get to be her age."

"Your cousin live around here?" asked Nate. He watched the Winter X Games religiously each year, and was familiar with most of the snowboard competitors. There was only one person from Vermont, and it was a dude—Cory Rainier.

"No, she lives in Colorado."

"Oh, the *other* 'Green Mountain State,'" Nate said, elbowing me in the ribs. "Get it?" I snickered.

"Yeah, I get it," I said. The kid looked at us skeptically.

"Is that about weed?" he asked. Nate and I froze.

"No," I said a little too quickly.

"*Pfft,* what?" Nate's voice was a little higher than normal. "Of course not. It was about, you know—" He elbowed me again for support.

"Ecology," I stammered. Nate rolled his eyes. But I was committed. "You know, uh, forests. The environment."

"The environment," Nate repeated with a forced smile. He turned around so his back was against the counter and whispered, "Dumbass," in my ear.

"It's okay if it was about weed," the kid said without missing a beat, completely ignoring my horrible coverup. "I know about that stuff."

"Oh yeah?" Nate said, looking over his shoulder at him. "What do you know about weed?"

"Nate, he's like, eight," I said, trying to avoid this conversation.

"Actually, I'm gonna be nine tomorrow," the kid said cheerfully. "And I know that marijuana is bad but sometimes it can help people who are sick. Like my uncle. He has cancer."

"Of course he does," I muttered, and this time Nate slapped me upside the head.

"Sorry," I mumbled. I was just sick of thinking about cancer. The boy stared at me thoughtfully as he fiddled with the paper his sticker had been on.

Nate kept talking to the kid about snowboarding while I excused myself to the inventory room. I pretended that another order had come through just so I could sit down at Andrea's desk for a couple of minutes. I rubbed my eyes until I saw stars. *Get your shit together*, I told myself. *Your shift's almost over.*

I went back out to the floor and found the store empty of customers. The little boy's parents had come and gotten him. Nate was getting started on the closing tasks for the night. He hardly looked up from the checklist he was scanning.

"The kid left that for you," he said, nodding at a crumpled paper on the counter.

But when I got closer, I saw it wasn't just a crumpled piece of paper. It was the sticker back, folded carefully into a paper airplane. I picked it up gingerly, as if it might disintegrate in my fingers. I held it up to my face, examining the creases. I heard Wilder's laugh floating through the air, spiraling up to the rafters. It weaved in and out of itself, creating loops out of the whimsical sound waves.

A reflexive smile spread across my face as I gently set the airplane down on the counter.

eleven

September 4, 2014 was a chilly, cloudy autumn morning. The leaves outside Burlington High School were still green, the manicured lawn covered in dew that soaked our socks as we shuffled across it. It was the start of our junior year, over a year after Wilder had been declared NED. Her peach fuzz hair had grown to the longest it would ever be since her initial diagnosis—a whopping 2.5 centimeters, thanks to the maintenance chemotherapy.

She wasn't worried about her short hair, though. She never cared about her physical appearance. When you beat cancer, your priorities get reorganized. Looks don't mean much if you're dead, so Wilder's priorities rested on living.

It was Wilder's last first day of high school, although we didn't know that at the time. But I remember everything about that day.

She was wearing her brother's faded, cobalt blue ECHO Aquarium shirt, the sleeves almost touching her elbows. A pair of beige chino shorts stopped just above her knees, and black Guinness crew socks—which would get her in trouble by the end of the day—reached halfway up her calf. Her maroon Vans were in pristine condition aside from the dew absorbed by the canvas.

We snuck into the building through the band door to avoid the faculty members cheerfully greeting students. We were dreading the school year. We had to take the SATs later that fall and start thinking about colleges. I felt dizzy imagining the future. Wilder was wary about planning so far in advanced. Rightfully so, I guess.

"You're a scrub," she muttered under her breath as we passed people we didn't like. I led the way, using my stature to clear a path for us through the packed hallways. "You're a bitch. You're actually cool. Oh my god, you didn't graduate?"

"Wilder," I said over my shoulder, trying not to laugh so I wouldn't encourage her.

"What?" she asked, almost offended that I had even considered calling her out.

"Let's just try to make this a good year," I said appeasingly. She rolled her eyes.

"Okay, Gandhi," she snapped.

We arrived at our first period class, United States History with Mr. Figueroa. We sat down next to each other, dreading the prospect of starting each morning with a class that was sure to bore us. The bell rang, and Mr. Figueroa walked in. He was a rotund man with a bald spot in the center of his head and perpetually sweaty armpits. He had on a Pokemon tie, to which Wilder immediately grinned and whispered to me, "It's gonna be a good year with this guy."

Figueroa passed out our syllabus, talking about his expectations for us and outlining what we would be learning. I zoned out, and in my inattentiveness, folded the syllabus into a paper airplane.

"Hey," Wilder poked me with her pencil. "Teach me how to do that." I raised my eyebrows at her.

"You don't know how to make a paper airplane?"

"Never learned," she replied with a casual shrug.

So as Figueroa droned on about plagiarism and what percentage of our grade was made up by class participation, I showed Wilder how to fold a paper airplane. And when Figueroa turned around to write on the board, Wilder launched her airplane across the room. It hit Seamus Giles in the shoulder, and he searched for the culprit. Declan Frost pointed at Wilder's shit-eating grin, and the two of them hastily folded their syllabi into airplanes to launch a counterattack. Declan's flew off course, landing smoothly on top of Stephanie Valencia's notebook. Startled at first, she quickly caught on to what we were up to, and she sent the airplane to the back corner of the room. It nose-dived into a sleeping Brett Morley, which Nevaeh Wolfe then scooped up and sent back to Wilder.

Mr. Figueroa was none the wiser.

For the first three quarters of the school year, our class launched airstrikes on one another while Figueroa lectured us, his eyes always downcast since he constantly referred to his notes. Quiet snickers and stifled giggles kept us all awake. Sometimes we would write notes on the wings of the airplanes, other times we would decorate the crafts with highlighters and simple sketches.

But when Wilder relapsed, she had to stop going to school. And after a couple days, the airplanes stopped. The class grew quiet and dull. Her absence from the desk next to me was noticeable. Even Figueroa realized something was amiss, though he never said anything. But he would pause during his lectures more often, and when he did, he would actually look up at us. He would thoughtfully scan the crowd of students, as if searching for some sign of life. We just sat there, disengaged, wishing we were back in bed, avoiding our responsibilities. Avoiding our realities.

*   *   *   *   *

While Mr. Figueroa's first period history class may have stopped constructing paper airplanes, Wilder Murray did not. As she spent hours that turned into days in the hospital, she had to fill her time somehow. Between Netflix and sketching and painting, Wilder also folded paper airplanes. She would wait for a nurse to start to walk through the door and then launch it at them, hoping to hit them square in the chest. More often than not, she missed. Regardless, it put a smile on the attending nurse's face and made Wilder laugh.

June 2, 2015 was a clear afternoon. Wilder and I planned on going for a walk in the garden later, after we had gotten frozen yogurt from the cafeteria. She was sitting cross-legged on her bed, hooked up to the IV pole. I was sitting in an arm chair next to her, playing a game on my phone. She had been sketching in her notepad for a few minutes beforehand, but I guess she had switched to folding a paper airplane, because suddenly one landed between my phone and my chest.

I smiled.

"Dude," I said, throwing it back to her. It landed in her lap, and she stared at it for a long time.

"You know, when you think about it," she said slowly. "People are kind of like paper airplanes."

I put my phone down.

"Huh?"

"People are fragile, like paper airplanes," she explained, holding it up in the space between us. "We crumple easily. Our wings get bent, and we don't always fly straight." She aimed the airplane at an undistinguished spot on the window and let it go. It nose-dived into the tile floor long before it could reach the glass.

"We're nowhere close to being invincible. And we don't really have control over where we end up. But we're resilient. No matter how many times we crash, or how wrinkled our wings get, we flatten ourselves out and fly again." Wilder picked at the fabric of the blanket she was sitting on.

She looked up at me.

"We can try again."

And for the first time in six years, there were tears in her blue-green eyes.

They stayed put, glass prisms distorting the swirling hurricane beneath them.

She smiled at me, the same shit-eating grin she had the first time she made a paper airplane. But the tears stayed in her eyes, unable to be blinked away. I grabbed her hand, and she squeezed it, tight, as if she was afraid I would fly away.

Oh, the irony.

twelve

I thought I knew what it meant to grieve. I had lost two grandparents and an uncle before, so I felt pretty confident in my grieving abilities. But Wilder proved me extremely wrong.

Her death, when I first found out it finally happened, was a swift kick to the groin. Even though I had known for weeks that it was coming, I was still shocked. No matter how many times I said, "Wilder is dying," I truly believed—albeit unconsciously—that she would recover. That she would wake up in the morning and pluck the vital monitors off, and climb out of bed without the pain of tumors riddling her body. And she would have hair again, long hair that reached her shoulders, and she would walk to UVM with us and we would lay in the grass under a blue sky, and we would all be happy again. Genuinely happy.

Yeah, that's what I thought would happen.

But instead, I got a text from Pete Murray. It just said, "She's gone." It was up to me to tell the others. I texted the group chat as my chest heaved and my eyes burned and my throat collapsed in on itself. The messages came in one by one, the screen blurry from tears that had fallen on it. Somehow it was decided we would go to the aquarium. I let myself cry for another hour, then managed to get myself together. I met Amari at my car. We drove in silence down to the harbor.

I thought you could only feel that raw, shocking pain once. After all, you can only find out a person is dead one time. Once you know it, that's it. You can't be hurt in that way again. But I was wrong about that, too.

After Wilder died, I started having nightmares. I can't remember what they were all about, but I know they were extremely stressful. One nightmare that I had over and over again was about the day she died. In it, I found out she was dead for the first time. And it was up to me to tell every single individual that cared about her, in person. So in my own fresh pain, I had to watch everyone else absorb the news and break down.

And then I would wake up, my heart thudding in my constricted chest; my eyes damp with tears first thing in the morning; my throat on fire from desperate screams that never escaped.

Nights featuring those dreams left me drained. I found myself taking a nap almost every day to compensate. But the naps were just as restless. Sleep quickly became my enemy.

To try to comfort myself during those mornings where it felt like I had found out about Wilder's death for the first time, I would think about how this isn't day one—she's been gone for a while, and I was handling it. But as it turns out, it doesn't really help to think about how long she's been gone. So then the only solution would be to not think about Wilder at all. Which is impossible.

Grief is a hell you can never escape from.

It doesn't get better with time. When Wilder first died, it was like someone had shot a bullet through a sheet of metal, leaving a jagged hole with sharp edges that cut the tips of your fingers if you dare to touch them. As time goes on, that hole doesn't close up on its own. The dangerous edges don't mend themselves, but they do get dulled down. Not by the passing of time, but by your own personal strength.

Grief never goes away. It subsides, retreats from the surface and settles into your bones as a lead lining, weighing you down just enough to let you know that it's there. But then there are days, random and intermittent, when it bursts out to the forefront. It forces you to acknowledge it. It forces you to feel.

But regardless of the presence of grief in my life, I survived.

Because at the end of the day, the world keeps going, with or without you. It doesn't stop for anyone, no matter how broken you may feel. The universe doesn't care if you aren't the same person you were last week— it's going to keep operating at its mystical pace, and you have a choice: move along with it, or drown in your own sorrow.

I decided I will never be okay that Wilder is gone. I don't need to be, quite frankly. However, I do have to keep going, because she always kept going, even when the odds were stacked against her. I have to keep living, because if Wilder had the choice, she would have kept living, too.

thirteen

My legs dangled over the pier's concrete edge, the sneakers on my feet casting long shadows over the water. The waves rippled towards me, rising up as far as the lake would allow them, then settling down and smoothing out for a moment. Overhead, seagulls circled in search of food. Down the shoreline, children squealed as they chased each other around. It was one of the last days of summer, and Burlington was bustling.

The college students had come back for the fall semester, increasing the city's population. They milled about during their free time, visiting the cafés and ice cream stands that cropped up around the harbor. Business was booming at my parents' Ben & Jerry's. Life was continuing—blossoming.

But I felt stuck, frozen in a block of ice. I couldn't sleep peacefully knowing that Wilder was gone. With each week that passed, it seemed less real. How could she just be gone?

Wilder liked practical jokes—she loved messing with her friends. Surely, she was just joking around with us. I would walk into school on the first day of senior year, and she'd be sitting in class, waiting for me with her wide grin. And she'd say, "I got you, oh, you should've seen the look on your face at the funeral. You're such a scrub!"

I thought maybe if I screamed loud enough, her voice would break through mine and I would be able to hear her again.

I thought that maybe, if I squinted just right, I could see her standing on the sidewalk, a backwards baseball cap protecting her bald head from the scorching sun.

And maybe if I closed my eyes hard enough, I could transport myself to wherever Wilder was. And we could sit and laugh together, just the two of us. Even if it was only for five minutes. Or all of eternity. I would be okay with leaving my life behind for her.

I just want her back.

I said that more often now: in my head, to Amari and Jessa, to my mom. When I said it to myself, my brain lied to me. It said, *maybe.*

When I said it to Amari and Jessa, they looked at me with sad eyes and nodded in agreement. Because they knew the truth, but they felt the same way.

When I said it to my mom, her voice raised a pitch and she would say, "That's not possible, Knox, you just have to move on."

It was agonizing.

Crying didn't help anymore. It made me feel nauseous. And it wasn't going to achieve anything. Tears wouldn't bring Wilder back.

Nothing would.

It hurt to think about that. It felt like someone was punching me in the gut with a fist covered in acid. It tore through me, eating away at my insides. A dark voice in the back of my head taunted, *you'll never hear her laugh again, you'll never see her in this lifetime. You'll grow old and you'll forget how she sounded, what her hugs felt like, what her eyes looked like in the sunlight. You'll forget Wilder.*

I didn't want to forget Wilder. That was my biggest fear. That I would forget that day in June, when she squeezed my hand so tightly. Or one of those days in July, towards the end of her life, when she was mostly unconscious. And I was laying next to her, and she nuzzled her head on my shoulder and slipped her cold hand into mine, and her peach fuzz hair tickled my cheek. Or all those times we would be hanging out, and she would flick me in the ear, because it always got under my skin and she liked to see me get pissed for no reason.

Every day, I imagined her wide, toothy grin, the way her nose crinkled and how her eyes narrowed so they were almost closed. I replayed conversations in my mind on a loop so I wouldn't forget how she sounded, her husky voice that squeaked whenever she got excited about something. The way she would mock people out by adopting a new persona.

The rest of the world was moving on. And I knew that Wilder didn't want me to just exist, to barely get by. She wanted me to *live*. To live the life she never got the chance to experience.

But did she know how fucking difficult that was?

*   *   *   *   *

The day Matt Descoteaux came into our lives, Amari, Wilder, Jessa, and I were hanging out behind the aquarium. We were on the last of a pack of Marlboro's we had stolen from Jessa's stepdad, so we were passing it between us. Matt sauntered up to us, seemingly out of nowhere, and asked if he could take a hit.

"Dude, it's a cigarette," Wilder said. But she held it out to him anyway. Matt shook his head and pushed it away.

"Sorry, I thought it was a joint," he explained. Wilder looked him up and down.

"You thought you could just walk up to a group of teenagers you don't know and ask to take a hit of that good kush?" She said it like he was insane. Matt stared back at her coolly.

"I mean, you offered the cigarette to a guy you don't know, so I probably wasn't too far off."

Amari and I exchanged glances. We watched for Wilder's reaction. After a moment, she smirked.

"What's your name, stranger?" she asked.

"Matthieu," he answered. "Matthieu Descoteaux."

"Ooh, a baguette man," Wilder giggled with a horribly fake French accent, and we all laughed, Matt included.

That was it. From then on, Matt was in our core group of friends. He was a year older than us, newly emigrated from Canada. He got us fake ID's and hooked us up with a new weed dealer.

That was when Wilder was alive.

After Wilder died, he drifted away from us. He played basketball with Amari once in a while, but that was it. I didn't hold it against Matt, I figured we all grieve in our own way, so why should I judge? But I'd be lying if I said it didn't sting. It was a slap in the face, to lose not just one but two friends.

It made Wilder's death feel less real, too. It made it seem as though Wilder was just ghosting us. Like she had drifted away or was giving us the cold shoulder. She was still alive, leading a separate life somewhere. But if I called her phone, she would answer.

Except, she wouldn't.

Her phone had been turned off yesterday.

Cynthia had told me earlier in the morning, when I went over to pick up Crew for basketball. She gave me a copy of the last bill that showed activity on Wilder's phone. It gave the text message count over the course of 30 days, and broke it down by number. Wilder had texted my number the most—17,164 times.

The next bill period started just a week before Wilder died. She was hardly on her phone then. But she had still texted my number the most—202 times. The last text message she ever sent was on July 18, 2015. Two days before she died.

I had a copy of that bill, too. I don't know why Cynthia thought I would want these things. For proof of my friendship with her daughter? I didn't ask. I just numbly took the papers, folded them up and slid them in my pocket. I didn't say a single word to Crew. I pretended like everything was fine.

But now, with my legs hanging over the edge, my forehead grazing the safety rope, I took out the most recent bill. I stared at that number one last time, the ink blurring before me. Deliberately, I folded it in half.

Flattened it out.

Folded the top two corners to the center.

Folded the paper in half again, along the initial crease.

Folded the wings over just enough to touch the bottom of the crease.

And again, folded the wings over one final time.

I ran my hand along the plane, straightening out the nose. Holding it between my thumb and first two fingers, I aimed it at a sailboat off in the horizon. I pulled back my arm and launched it into the air. It spiraled up, did a little flip in the wind, and then traveled forward, heading to the left of where I had intended it to go.

I watched as the paper airplane nose-dived into the lake about fifteen feet away from me. It slipped under the surface, floating in limbo somewhere in the Champlain.

fourteen

Wilder wasn't ready to die. I think that's what makes all of this so unfair. After everything she had been through—the surgeries, the radiation, the harsh chemotherapies that left her with horrendous side effects, doctors and nurses waking her up at all hours of the night to administer medications, countless needle pokes, the pain and nausea, hair and weight loss, altered taste buds, the hope that came with being declared NED only to relapse almost two years later—she never wished for death. Giving up was never a thought that crossed her mind. She loved life.

Wilder had a passion for living hard and fast. Not because death was waiting for her around the next bend; she had lived on the edge for as long as I'd known her, even before cancer. I guess she always knew how tragically short life is.

She never let the tragedy of her illness get in the way of her general happiness. She made jokes that would have been in poor taste if she herself wasn't plagued with the disease. She laughed about death as if to challenge it. It wasn't a defense mechanism. Rather, it was her way of acknowledging that death is as much a part of life as living is. And to live in fear of death is to not live at all.

Wilder had acquaintances, she had friends, she had boyfriends, and then she had me. I was lucky to have met her in sixth grade, back when I was shy and she was considered bossy. We spent our formative years together, navigating the waters of middle school and growing into ourselves. We changed a lot in six years, going from awkward, emo preteens to less emo degenerates that pissed off the baby boomer generation.

If it wasn't for Wilder telling me band kids grow up to live in their parents' basement and never get laid, I probably would have kept on playing the clarinet and stayed in my limited comfort zone. I would have been too scared to smoke weed, too worried about my "good Christian boy" reputation to drink. I would have never had the balls to ask Stephanie Valencia to prom, or snowboarded down the highest mountain Vermont has to offer. I would have never learned how to live if it wasn't for Wilder.

I don't just consider her to be my best friend. She had become my sister. And some people think that's odd, that after all the time I spent with her I never developed feelings for her. But that's the other thing Wilder taught me: guys and girls can be friends without it being weird. Wilder never "friendzoned" me; we had a mutual, unspoken understanding that a relationship between us would be catastrophic, because she was uncontainable, destructive, and unpredictable. And as friends, I loved that about her. It made her who she was, and I respected her for it. But for as outgoing as Wilder taught me to be, I still rely on some level of stability.

Like I said before, Wilder was an enigma just as much as she was an open book. Her unpredictability and penchant for hiding her emotions made her difficult to figure out. But she told you when she was taking a shit, whether or not you asked. If you ever dated her, nothing you did or said to her was private—I was told every detail while the two of us sat in the parking lot of McDonalds eating fries, Wilder's bare feet on my dashboard as she affectionately talked trash about you.

And since she was so aware of how short life was, she was never heartbroken. Not even when Brady Pratt broke up with her, the only guy she told "I love you" to first rather than him saying it. Watching romantic comedies and eating ice cream out of the pint wasn't Wilder's style after a break up. She didn't care enough; in her opinion, a break up was the universe's way of telling her it wasn't the right guy for her, and she took that in stride.

We didn't talk much about relationships towards the end, or whether she was sad that she would never find her "soulmate" and get married. I think when Wilder realized she was dying, she chose not to think about the things she would never get to do or accomplish. Because focusing her energy on that would be to distract from the good things in her life, as minimal as that list had become.

I don't know what Wilder was thinking at the end. We didn't talk about our feelings really, and we kept the sentimental stuff to a minimum. Part of me desperately wants to know, to unlock the secrets of her mind. I think that's the thing I miss the most about Wilder: her mind.

If I'm going to use simple adjectives to describe her, Wilder was witty. Outgoing. Adventurous. Sarcastic. Daring. Impulsive. Proud. Empathetic. Outspoken. Stubborn. Carefree, or at least as carefree as she could be.

But basic words don't do Wilder nearly enough justice. She was so much more than words. She was brilliant, not in the book smarts sense but in the sense that everything she did, when added up into one lump sum, was pure magic. Her art, her perspective, her way of verbalizing things that we look to classical writers to explain or justify, all of that made her exceptional. Wilder was wise well beyond her years, with talent and beauty and love that made the world better off having her in it. And without her, well, nothing seems to make sense.

I don't know if she ever truly grasped what an impact she had on people, or even just me. You see, Wilder and I talked about pretty much everything in our lives together. We dreamed together. If I ever had a problem, Wilder is who I talked to. Not Amari, who I had been raised with. Not my parents, not Meadow, not anyone else. Wilder was it.

Her perspective on life and timely advice makes her death that much more severe, because I no longer have my confidant. Not only that, but Wilder did so much for me. She got me out of my comfort zone. She introduced me to music that led to some of the best live shows I've ever seen.

But most of all, Wilder taught me to live fearlessly and love endlessly. And that's not to say that we lived recklessly; we didn't get into high speed chases with the cops or do stupid shit that would result in irreparable harm. No, we lived without fear when it was possible: fear of the unknown, fear of failure, fear of rejection, fear of judgement, fear of pain.

And we loved endlessly. Wilder was never afraid to tell the people she cared about that she loved them. Whether that was verbally, through a lengthy text, or just a, "Drive safe, asshole," she showed her love. Life is far, far too short to not show your appreciation for the people in your life.

I don't want you to think that I'm immortalizing Wilder in gold, as if she wasn't flawed. She was not perfect. She broke laws, she made mistakes, she let her hardheadedness ruin several relationships within her family and friend group over the years. Her convictions sometimes got in the way of her compassion. Her brutal honesty resulted in hurt feelings, and the tough love that I had grown accustomed to was not always viewed as a positive attribute.

But Wilder's flaws made her who she was. And that was a voracious, unapologetic vortex that destroyed everything in her wake. She smashed all of us to pieces while she was alive, shattering every expectation and preconception we had of the world. She was mercurial and brash, making her intimidating to anyone who didn't know her very well. And in death, she decimated us again, tearing us apart as we were forced to live without her.

I've only been able to write this eulogy, the one she deserved, a year after her death. One year hasn't made the pain go away. It's just changed, and instead of burning and suffocating, it's buried itself deep within me, settling into an ache. My empty passenger seat still reminds me of the loss, carrying memories of Wilder dancing to trap music and screaming lyrics at the top of her lungs out the window, or the time she hid a Four Loko under her leg when we got stopped by the police, or the countless head slaps she hit me with when I zoned out while at red lights.

365 days hasn't made me stop picking up my phone to call Wilder's disconnected number and ask her about her day or tell her about mine. Each time I think about calling her, I remember when she hung up on me because I said Kendrick Lamar was a better rapper than J. Cole. Or all the times she would

start singing hits of the 2000s when she was in isolation in the hospital because her immune system was nonexistent.

But in the course of this one year, I've seen proof that she's still around. I don't pray to a deity, but I do ask Wilder to have my back when things get tough, or when I need an extra boost of confidence. And more often than not, she pulls through for me.

Wilder was of the mentality that when things happen, good or bad, it's the universe's way of steering us in the right direction. I personally believe that when things happen now, it's Wilder acting—and I trust Wilder more than anyone, so I know she's got my back, and won't put me into situations that I can't get through.

It's been a year without Wilder on Earth, and I swear the planet has felt the effects of her absence. The world has seemed a bit more grey, and I still feel weighed down. There isn't a day that goes by that I don't think about her, about how much I miss having her around. But I am trying to live more like her, giving less fucks and putting myself out there. Picking myself up when I nose-dive like a paper airplane. Laughing at every opportunity. Loving without hesitation.

Seventeen years was not an adequate lifetime for Wilder, and it's the furthest thing from fair that she didn't get more. But I am grateful for the six years I got to spend with her as my partner in crime. To be able to call Wilder my friend has been a privilege, and knowing that I've got such a badass for a guardian angel is quite the honor.

Thank you for everything, Wilder Murray.

A comparative adjective that will never be matched, certainly not in this lifetime.

I love you.

There are dozens of books on grief, but none on What To Do When Your Best Friend Gets Murdered.

Victoria Brooks, who is credited with the quote at the beginning of this book, got 18 years, five months, and four days on this earth before her life, along with her mother's, was cut far too short.

Suddenly, my life was no longer linear. It became divided into two parts, Before Victoria's death and After. Before, I was a skeptic, but I held a thread of idealism between my fingers and believed in the ultimate good of humanity. After, I was knocked on my ass. Any shred of faith in human decency was incinerated. Victoria was the most genuine, kindhearted, and down to earth friend I had—she, like Wilder, was brilliant. How could someone have so much malice to end such a beautiful life?

Victoria's death left me grasping for straws. My mom, who has read practically every book on grief, admitted that she had no words to help me. There are grief books, and there are

146

parenting books, but neither offer a blueprint of how to comfort your kid when their best friend is killed. It happened over Thanksgiving break, three days before I was supposed to return to school 250 miles away. I went back to Albany, where I spent an inordinate amount of time in my room, alone, sobbing and reading Victoria's poetry.

Victoria's death impacted me in ways that I could have never expected. To me, my friends and family seemed less affected. I felt as though they were just going on with their lives while I was left to cope. English singer Declan McKenna says it best in his song "Paracetamol" - *The world will keep on turning, even if we're not the same.* But in reality, my friends and family were impacted significantly by Victoria's death. It changed how we all viewed the world, and for me, it changed how I chose to live my life.

There is no timeline for grief. But people still expect you to get better, to stop being sad. The adage, "Time heals all wounds," plays a big part in this. But that phrase is bullshit.

The jagged hole KJ references never heals. The rough edges smooth over, but the hole never closes. It never repairs itself. The pain of initial grief subsides from a chaotic, oppressive, burning to a soreness that nestles in your bones. Grief doesn't heal or get better: it just changes form.

So why did I write this book? In part, it was a form of catharsis. I wrote the book I needed to help myself.

But I started this book long before Victoria died. Seven months before Victoria's murder, a Vine star named Emma Greer passed away after battling cancer. It was March 27, 2016. She was sixteen years old, with friends dedicated to remembering her. Her closest friends poured their hearts out on social media to express how much Greer meant to them, and the impact she had on them. I began writing *Paper Airplanes*, under a different title, shortly after Greer's death. I was inspired by her friends' determination to immortalize her.

I stopped writing *Paper Airplanes* when I got to college that September. But I started up again in February 2017, a little less than three months after Victoria died. It was no longer just about Greer; it was about the pain I experienced when I lost Victoria, who had been a constant presence in my life since I met her.

Paper Airplanes got its title from the metaphor Wilder describes in this book. That metaphor was something I came up with when I graduated high school, when I witnessed the fragility and resilience of a close friend that was engaging in self-destructive behavior.

I described the metaphor to Victoria. I wanted to get a paper airplane tattooed on my arm, so I tested the idea on her first. She got quiet, and I assumed she hated it. Then she said, "I love it. Do you want to get matching tattoos?" I said yes.

Three months after Victoria died, I got my tattoo. When people asked about the meaning behind it, I told them there was a deeper story, but that only a few people close to me knew it. I just explained that it was a tribute to my friend who had passed away. Now, I guess the meaning behind my tattoo is at the world's disposal.

The hectic, raw, contradictory-at-times pain that KJ feels throughout the book is very real. I know it firsthand. Grief is not clear cut; it is not systematic. It comes in waves: some small ripples, some giant tsunamis. It debilitates your mind's infrastructure. And if you let it, it can consume you.

It is Wilder's hope for KJ that he will move forward, not on. As KJ comes to know, Wilder wants him to live for her—to live the life she'll never have the opportunity to experience. That is moving forward. And just as KJ laments, it's a difficult task to undertake. But it is a necessary one; it would be a disservice not to live for those who don't get the chance.

KJ, like myself, will never just "move on"—we will never forget the friends we lost, the memories we share with them. And like KJ, my biggest fear is that I will forget Victoria's voice. The way she articulated each word whenever she read her poems aloud. Or how she would serenade me with Kanye West over the phone during our hours-long conversations.

I'll leave it at this: if you are reading this book while grieving the loss of a loved one, I hope you can find solace in knowing that KJ lives for Wilder—passionately, ambitiously, and deliberately. I myself am trying to do just that. I felt compelled to publish this book as a step in my process of moving forward, with the hope that it might help others facing unbearable grief.

acknowledgments

Thank you to:

My dad, also known as my incredibly hardworking (read: overworked) editor, for going above and beyond for his kids, and for believing in us no matter what.

My mom, for everything she does for our family and for always being a phone call away.

My brothers, Josh and Nick, for their unending support and love.

Emma Greer DiBiase, for her hilarious videos and lasting legacy.

Joe, my brother from another mother, for supporting every writing endeavor and encouraging my (sometimes poor) life decisions. Thank you for always listening and having my back, even from 250 miles away.

Anyone who has ever read a single word I've written.

Frank Ocean, Kendrick Lamar, and J. Cole (in that order).

And finally:

Thank you for everything, Victoria Brooks.

A beautiful and talented friend that will never be matched, certainly not in this lifetime.

I love you.

about the author

In addition to writing books, Hannah Olin is the Undisputed Dance Champ of her high school psychology class. She is most comfortable in a pair of Vans, which she wore when she was featured on the Teen Author Panel at the 2016 Greater Rochester Teen Book Fest. Her Twitter account @HannahOlin is mostly dedicated to memes, mishaps, and Frank Ocean.